Bones in London

Bones in London

Edgar Wallace

MINT EDITIONS

Bones in London was first published in 1915.

This edition published by Mint Editions 2020.

ISBN 9781513266404 | E-ISBN 9781513266848

Published by Mint Editions®

MINT
EDITIONS

minteditionbooks.com

Publishing Director: Jennifer Newens
Project Manager: Gabrielle Maudiere
Design & Production: Rachel Lopez Metzger
Typesetting: Westchester Publishing Services

Contents

Chapter 1

Bones and Big Business

There was a slump in the shipping market, and men who were otherwise decent citizens wailed for one hour of glorious war, when Kenyon Line Deferred had stood at 88½, and even so poor an organization as Siddons Steam Packets Line had been marketable at 3⅜.

Two bareheaded men came down the busy street, their hands thrust into their trousers pockets, their sleek, well-oiled heads bent in dejection.

No word they spoke, keeping step with the stern precision of soldiers. Together they wheeled through the open doors of the Commercial Trust Building, together they left-turned into the elevator, and simultaneously raised their heads to examine its roof, as though in its panelled ceiling was concealed some Delphic oracle who would answer the riddle which circumstances had set them.

They dropped their heads together and stood with sad eyes, regarding the attendant's leisurely unlatching of the gate. They slipped forth and walked in single file to a suite of offices inscribed "Pole Brothers, Brokers," and, beneath, "The United Merchant Shippers' Corporation," and passed through a door which, in addition to this declaration, bore the footnote "Private."

Here the file divided, one going to one side of a vast pedestal desk and one to the other. Still with their hands pushed deep into their pockets, they sank, almost as at a word of command, each into his cushioned chair, and stared at one another across the table.

They were stout young men of the middle thirties, clean-shaven and ruddy. They had served their country in the late War, and had made many sacrifices to the common cause. One had worn uniform and one had not. Joe had occupied some mysterious office which permitted and, indeed, enjoined upon him the wearing of the insignia of captain, but had forbidden him to leave his native land. The other had earned a little decoration with a very big title as a buyer of boots for Allied nations. Both had subscribed largely to War Stock, and a reminder of their devotion to the cause of liberty was placed to their credit every half-year.

But for these, war, with its horrific incidents, its late hours, its midnight railway journeys by trains on which sleeping berths could not be had for love or money, its food cards and statements of excess profits, was past. The present held its tragedy so poignant as to overshadow that breathless terrifying moment when peace had come and found the firm with the sale of the Fairy Line of cargo steamers uncompleted, contracts unsigned, and shipping stock which had lived light-headedly in the airy spaces, falling deflated on the floor of the house.

The Fairy Line was not a large line. It was, in truth, a small line. It might have been purchased for two hundred thousand pounds, and nearly was. To-day it might be acquired for one hundred and fifty thousand pounds, and yet it wasn't.

"Joe," said the senior Mr. Pole, in a voice that came from his varnished boots, "we've got to do something with Fairies."

"Curse this War!" said Joe in cold-blooded even tones. "Curse the Kaiser! A weak-kneed devil who might at least have stuck to it for another month! Curse him for making America build ships, curse him for——"

"Joe," said the stout young man on the other side of the table, shaking his head sadly, "it is no use cursing, Joe. We knew that they were building ships, but the business looked good to me. If Turkey hadn't turned up her toes and released all that shipping——"

"Curse Turkey!" said the other, with great calmness. "Curse the Sultan and Enver and Taalat, curse Bulgaria and Ferdinand——"

"Put in one for the Bolsheviks, Joe," said his brother urgently, "and I reckon that gets the lot in trouble. Don't start on Austria, or we'll find ourselves cursing the Jugo-Slavs."

He sighed deeply, pursed his lips, and looked at his writing-pad intently.

Joe and Fred Pole had many faults, which they freely admitted, such as their generosity, their reckless kindness of heart, their willingness to do their worst enemies a good turn, and the like. They had others which they never admitted, but which were none the less patent to their prejudiced contemporaries.

But they had virtues which were admirable. They were, for example, absolutely loyal to one another, and were constant in their mutual admiration and help. If Joe made a bad deal, Fred never rested until he had balanced things against the beneficiary. If Fred in a weak moment paid a higher price to the vendor of a property than he, as promoter, could afford, it was Joe who took the smug vendor out to dinner and, by persuasion, argument, and the frank expression of his liking for the unfortunate man, tore away a portion of his ill-gotten gains.

"I suppose," said Joe, concluding his minatory exercises, and reaching for a cigar from the silver box which stood on the table midway between the two, "I suppose we couldn't hold Billing to his contract. Have you seen Cole about it, Fred?"

The other nodded slowly.

"Cole says that there is no contract. Billing offered to buy the ships, and meant to buy them, undoubtedly; but Cole says that if you took Billing into court, the judge would chuck his pen in your eye."

"Would he now?" said Joe, one of whose faults was that he took things literally. "But perhaps if you took Billing out to dinner, Fred——"

"He's a vegetarian, Joe"—he reached in his turn for a cigar, snipped the end and lit it—"and he's deaf. No, we've got to find a sucker, Joe. I can sell the *Fairy May* and the *Fairy Belle*: they're little boats, and are worth money in the open market. I can sell the wharfage and offices and the goodwill——"

"What's the goodwill worth, Fred?"

"About fivepence net," said the gloomy Fred. "I can sell all these, but it is the *Fairy Mary* and the *Fairy Tilda* that's breaking my heart. And yet, Joe, there ain't two ships of their tonnage to be bought on the market. If you wanted two ships of the same size and weight, you couldn't buy 'em for a million—no, you couldn't. I guess they must be bad ships, Joe."

Joe had already guessed that.

"I offered 'em to Saddler, of the White Anchor," Fred went on, "and he said that if he ever started collecting curios he'd remember me. Then I tried to sell 'em to the Coastal Cargo Line—the very ships for the Newcastle and Thames river trade—and he said he couldn't think of it now that the submarine season was over. Then I offered 'em to young Topping, who thinks of running a line to the West Coast, but he said that he didn't believe in Fairies or Santa Claus or any of that stuff."

There was silence.

"Who named 'em *Fairy Mary* and *Fairy Tilda*?" asked Joe curiously.

"Don't let's speak ill of the dead," begged Fred; "the man who had 'em built is no longer with us, Joe. They say that joy doesn't kill, but that's a lie, Joe. He died two days after we took 'em over, and left all his money—all our money—to a nephew."

"I didn't know that," said Joe, sitting up.

"I didn't know it myself till the other day, when I took the deed of sale down to Cole to see if there wasn't a flaw in it somewhere. I've wired him."

"Who—Cole?"

"No, the young nephew. If we could only——"

He did not complete his sentence, but there was a common emotion and understanding in the two pairs of eyes that met.

"Who is he—anybody?" asked Joe vaguely.

Fred broke off the ash of his cigar and nodded.

"Anybody worth half a million is somebody, Joe," he said seriously. "This young fellow was in the Army. He's out of it now, running a business in the City—'Schemes, Ltd.,' he calls it. Lots of people know him—shipping people on the Coast. He's got a horrible nickname."

"What's that, Fred?"

"Bones," said Fred, in tones sufficiently sepulchral to be appropriate, "and, Joe, he's one of those bones I want to pick."

There was another office in that great and sorrowful City. It was perhaps less of an office than a boudoir, for it had been furnished on the higher plan by a celebrated firm of furnishers and decorators, whose advertisements in the more exclusive publications consisted of a set of royal arms, a photograph of a Queen Anne chair, and the bold surname of the firm. It was furnished with such exquisite taste that you could neither blame nor praise the disposition of a couch or the set of a purple curtain.

The oxydized silver grate, the Persian carpets, the rosewood desk, with its Venetian glass flower vase, were all in harmony with the panelled walls, the gentlemanly clock which ticked sedately on the Adam mantelpiece, the Sheraton chairs, the silver—or apparently so—wall sconces, the delicate electrolier with its ballet skirts of purple silk.

All these things were evidence of the careful upbringing and artistic yearnings of the young man who "blended" for the eminent firm of Messrs. Worrows, By Appointment to the King of Smyrna, His Majesty the Emperor——(the blank stands for an exalted name which had been painted out by the patriotic management of Worrows), and divers other royalties.

The young man who sat in the exquisite chair, with his boots elevated to and resting upon the olive-green leather of the rosewood writing-table, had long since grown familiar with the magnificence in which he moved and had his being. He sat chewing an expensive paper-knife of ivory, not because he was hungry, but because he was bored. He had entered into his kingdom brimful of confidence and with unimagined thousands of pounds to his credit in the coffers of the Midland and Somerset Bank.

He had brought with him a bright blue book, stoutly covered and brassily locked, on which was inscribed the word "Schemes."

That book was filled with writing of a most private kind and of a frenzied calculation which sprawled diagonally over pages, as for example:

Buy up old houses .... say	2,000	pounds.
Pull them down .... say	500	pounds.
Erect erect 50 Grand Flats .... say	10,000	pounds.
Paper, pante, windows, etc. .... say	1,000	pounds.
Total	12,000	pounds.
50 Flats let at 80 pounds per annum.	40,000	lbs.
Net profit .... say	50	per cent.

Note.—For good middel class familys steady steady people. By this means means doing good turn to working classes solving houseing problem and making money which can be distribbuted distribbutted to the poor.

Mr. Augustus Tibbetts, late of H.M. Houssa Rifles, was, as his doorplate testified, the Managing Director of "Schemes, Ltd." He was a severe looking young man, who wore a gold-rimmed monocle on his grey check waistcoat and occasionally in his left eye. His face was of that brick-red which spoke of a life spent under tropical suns, and when erect he conveyed a momentary impression of a departed militarism.

He uncurled his feet from the table, and, picking up a letter, read it through aloud—that is to say, he read certain words, skipped others, and substituted private idioms for all he could not or would not trouble to pronounce.

"Dear Sir," (he mumbled), "as old friends of your dear uncle, and so on and so forth, we are taking the first opportunity of making widdly widdly wee. . . Our Mr. Fred Pole will call upon you and place himself widdly widdly wee—tum tiddly um tum.—Yours truly."

Mr. Tibbetts frowned at the letter and struck a bell with unnecessary violence. There appeared in the doorway a wonderful man in scarlet breeches and green zouave jacket. On his head was a dull red tarbosh, on his feet scarlet slippers, and about his waist a sash of Oriental audacity. His face, large and placid, was black, and, for all his suggestiveness of the brilliant East, he was undoubtedly negroid.

The costume was one of Mr. Tibbetts's schemes. It was faithfully copied from one worn by a gentleman of colour who serves the Turkish coffee at the Wistaria Restaurant. It may be said that there was no special reason why an ordinary business man should possess a bodyguard at all, and less reason why he should affect one who had the appearance of a burlesque Othello, but Mr. Augustus Tibbetts, though a business man, was not ordinary.

"Bones"—for such a name he bore without protest in the limited circles of his friendship—looked up severely.

"Ali," he demanded, "have you posted the ledger?"

"Sir," said Ali, with a profound obeisance, "the article was too copious for insertion in aperture of collection box, so it was transferred to the female lady behind postal department counter."

Bones leapt up, staring.

"Goodness gracious, Heavens alive, you silly old ass—you—you haven't posted it—in the post?"

"Sir," said Ali reproachfully, "you instructed posting volume in exact formula. Therefore I engulfed it in wrappings and ligatures of string, and safely delivered it to posting authority."

Bones sank back in his chair.

"It's no use—no use, Ali," he said sadly, "my poor uncivilized savage, it's not your fault. I shall never bring you up to date, my poor silly old josser. When I say 'post' the ledger, I mean write down all the money you've spent on cabs in the stamp book. Goodness gracious alive! You can't run a business without system, Ali! Don't you know that, my dear old image? How the dooce do you think the auditors are to know how I spend my jolly old uncle's money if you don't write it down, hey? Posting means writing. Good Heavens"—a horrid thought dawned on him—"who did you post it to?"

"Lord," said Ali calmly, "destination of posted volume is your lordship's private residency."

Ali's English education had been secured in the laboratory of an English scientist in Sierra Leone, and long association with that learned man had endowed him with a vocabulary at once impressive and recondite.

Bones gave a resigned sigh.

"I'm expecting——" he began, when a silvery bell tinkled.

It was silvery because the bell was of silver. Bones looked up, pulled down his waistcoat, smoothed back his hair, fixed his eye-glass, and took up a long quill pen with a vivid purple feather.

"Show them in," he said gruffly.

"Them" was one well-dressed young man in a shiny silk hat, who, when admitted to the inner sanctum, came soberly across the room, balancing his hat.

"Ah, Mr. Pole—Mr. Fred Pole." Bones read the visitor's card with the scowl which he adopted for business hours. "Yes, yes. Be seated, Mr. Pole. I shall not keep you a minute."

He had been waiting all the morning for Mr. Pole. He had been weaving dreams from the letter-heading above Mr. Pole's letter.

Ships. . . ships. . . house-flags. . . brass-buttoned owners. . .

He waved Mr. Fred to a chair and wrote furiously. This frantic pressure of work was a phenomenon which invariably coincided with the arrival of a visitor. It was, I think, partly due to nervousness and partly to his dislike of strangers. Presently he finished, blotted the paper, stuck it in an envelope, addressed it, and placed it in his drawer. Then he took up the card.

"Mr. Pole?" he said.

"Mr. Pole," repeated that gentleman.

"Mr. *Fred* Pole?" asked Bones, with an air of surprise.

"Mr. Fred Pole," admitted the other soberly.

Bones looked from the card to the visitor as though he could not believe his eyes.

"We have a letter from you somewhere," he said, searching the desk. "Ah, here it is!" (It was, in fact, the only document on the table.) "Yes, yes, to be sure. I'm very glad to meet you."

He rose, solemnly shook hands, sat down again and coughed. Then he took up the ivory paper-knife to chew, coughed again as he detected the lapse, and put it down with a bang.

"I thought I'd like to come along and see you, Mr. Tibbetts," said Fred in his gentle voice; "we are so to speak, associated in business."

"Indeed?" said Bones. "In-deed?"

"You see, Mr. Tibbetts," Fred went on, with a sad smile, "your lamented uncle, before he went out of business, sold us his ships. He died a month later."

He sighed and Bones sighed.

"Your uncle was a great man, Mr. Tibbetts," he said, "one of the greatest business men in this little city. What a man!"

"Ah!" said Bones, shaking his head mournfully.

He had never met his uncle and had seldom heard of him. Saul Tibbetts was reputedly a miser, and his language was of such violence that the infant Augustus was invariably hurried to the nursery on such rare occasions as old Saul paid a family visit. His inheritance had come to Bones as in a dream, from the unreality of which he had not yet awakened.

"I must confess, Mr. Tibbetts," said Fred, "that I have often had qualms of conscience about your uncle, and I have been on the point of coming round to see you several times. This morning I said to my brother, 'Joe,' I said, 'I'm going round to see Tibbetts.' Forgive the familiarity, but we talk of firms like the Rothschilds and the Morgans without any formality."

"Naturally, naturally, naturally," murmured Bones gruffly.

"I said: 'I'll go and see Tibbetts and get it off my chest. If he wants those ships back at the price we paid for them, or even less, he shall have them.' 'Fred,' he said, 'you're too sensitive for business.' 'Joe,' I said, 'my conscience works even in business hours.'"

A light dawned on Bones and he brightened visibly.

"Ah, yes, my dear old Pole," he said almost cheerily, "I understand. You diddled my dear old uncle—bless his heart—out of money, and you want to pay it back. Fred"—Bones rose and extended his knuckly hand—"you're a jolly old sportsman, and you can put it there!"

"What I was going to say——" began Fred seriously agitated.

"Not a word. We'll have a bottle on this. What will you have—ginger-beer or cider?"

Mr. Fred suppressed a shudder with difficulty.

"Wait, wait, Mr. Tibbetts," he begged; "I think I ought to explain. We did not, of course, knowingly rob your uncle——"

"No, no, naturally," said Bones, with a facial contortion which passed for a wink. "Certainly not. We business men never rob anybody. Ali, bring the drinks!"

"We did not consciously rob him," continued Mr. Fred desperately, "but what we did do—— ah, this is my confession!"

"You borrowed a bit and didn't pay it back. Ah, naughty!" said Bones. "Out with the corkscrew, Ali. What shall it be—a cream soda or non-alcoholic ale?"

Mr. Fred looked long and earnestly at the young man.

"Mr. Tibbetts," he said, and suddenly grasped the hand of Bones, "I hope we are going to be friends. I like you. That's my peculiarity—I like people or I dislike them. Now that I've told you that we bought two ships from your uncle for one hundred and forty thousand pounds when we knew—yes, positively knew—they were worth at least twenty thousand pounds more—now I've told you this, I feel happier."

"Worth twenty thousand pounds more?" said Bones thoughtfully. Providence was working overtime for him, he thought.

"Of anybody's money," said Fred stoutly. "I don't care where you go, my dear chap. Ask Cole—he's the biggest shipping lawyer in this city—ask my brother, who, I suppose, is the greatest shipping authority in the world, or—what's the use of asking 'em?—ask yourself. If you're not Saul Tibbetts all over again, if you haven't the instinct and the eye and the brain of a shipowner—why, I'm a Dutchman! That's what I am—a Dutchman!"

He picked up his hat and his lips were pressed tight—a gesture and a grimace which stood for grim conviction.

"What are they worth to-day?" asked Bones, after a pause.

"What are they worth to-day?" Mr. Fred frowned heavily at the ceiling. "Now, what are they worth to-day? I forget how much I've spent on 'em—they're in dock now."

Bones tightened *his* lips, too.

"They're in dock now?" he said. He scratched his nose. "Dear old Fred Pole," he said, "you're a jolly old soul. By Jove that's not bad! 'Pole' an' 'soul' rhyme—did you notice it?"

Fred had noticed it.

"It's rum," said Bones, shaking his head, "it is rum how things get about. How did you know, old fellow-citizen, that I was going in for shippin'?"

Mr. Fred Pole did not know that Bones was going in for shipping, but he smiled.

"There are few things that happen in the City that I *don't* know," he admitted modestly.

"The Tibbetts Line," said Bones firmly, "will fly a house-flag of purple and green diagonally—that is, from corner to corner. There will be a yellow anchor in a blue wreath in one corner and a capital T in a red wreath in the other."

"Original, distinctly original," said Fred in wondering admiration. "Wherever did you get that idea?"

"I get ideas," confessed Bones, blushing, "some times in the night, sometimes in the day. The fleet"—Bones liked the sound of the word and repeated it—"the fleet will consist of the *Augustus*, the *Sanders*—a dear old friend of mine living at Hindhead—the *Patricia*—another dear old friend of mine living at Hindhead, too—in fact, in the same house. To tell you the truth, dear old Fred Pole, she's married to the other ship. And there'll be the *Hamilton*, another precious old soul, a very, very, very, very dear friend of mine who's comin' home shortly——"

"Well, what shall we say, Mr. Tibbetts?" said Fred, who had an early luncheon appointment. "Would you care to buy the two boats at the same price we gave your uncle for them?"

Bones rang his bell.

"I'm a business man, dear old Fred," said he soberly. "There's no time like the present, and I'll fix the matter—*now!*"

He said "now" with a ferociousness which was intended to emphasize his hard and inflexible business character.

Fred came into the private office of Pole & Pole after lunch that day, and there was in his face a great light and a peace which was almost beautiful.

But never beamed the face of Fred so radiantly as the countenance of the waiting Joe. He lay back in his chair, his cigar pointing to the ceiling.

"Well, Fred?"—there was an anthem in his voice.

"Very well, Joe." Fred hung up his unnecessary umbrella.

"I've sold the *Fairies*!"

Joe said it and Fred said it. They said it together. There was the same lilt of triumph in each voice, and both smiles vanished at the identical instant.

"*You've* sold the *Fairies*!" they said.

They might have been rehearsing this scene for months, so perfect was the chorus.

"Wait a bit, Joe," said Fred; "let's get the hang of this. I understand that you left the matter to me."

"I did; but, Fred, I was so keen on the idea I had that I had to nip in before you. Of course, I didn't go to him as Pole & Pole——"

"To him? What him?" asked Fred, breathing hard.

"To What's-his-name—Bones."

Fred took his blue silk handkerchief from his pocket and dabbed his face.

EDGAR WALLACE

"Go on, Joe," he said sadly

"I got him just before he went out to lunch. I sent up the United Merchant Shippers' card—it's our company, anyway. Not a word about Pole & Pole."

"Oh, no, of course not!" said Fred.

"And, my boy,"—this was evidently Joe's greatest achievement, for he described the fact with gusto—"not a word about the names of the ships. I just sold him two steamers, so and so tonnage, so and so classification——"

"For how much?"

Fred was mildly curious. It was the curiosity which led a certain political prisoner to feel the edge of the axe before it beheaded him.

"A hundred and twenty thousand!" cried Joe joyously. "He's starting a fleet, he says. He's calling it the Tibbetts Line, and bought a couple of ships only this morning."

Fred examined the ceiling carefully before he spoke.

"Joe," he said, "was it a firm deal? Did you put pen to paper?"

"You-bet-your-dear-sweet-life," said Joe, scornful at the suggestion that he had omitted such an indispensable part of the negotiation.

"So did I, Joe," said Fred. "Those two ships he bought were the two *Fairies*."

There was a dead silence.

"Well," said Joe uneasily, after a while, "we can get a couple of ships——"

"Where, Joe? You admitted yesterday there weren't two boats in the world on the market."

Another long silence.

"I did it for the best, Fred."

Fred nodded

"Something must be done. We can't sell a man what we haven't got. Joe, couldn't you go and play golf this afternoon whilst I wangle this matter out?"

Joe nodded and rose solemnly. He took down his umbrella from the peg and his shiny silk hat from another peg, and tiptoed from the room.

From three o'clock to four Mr. Fred Pole sat immersed in thought, and at last, with a big, heavy sigh, he unlocked his safe, took out his cheque-book and pocketed it.

Bones was on the point of departure, after a most satisfactory day's work, when Fred Pole was announced.

Bones greeted him like unto a brother—caught him by the hand at the very entrance and, still holding him thus, conducted him to one of his beautiful chairs.

"By Jove, dear old Fred," he babbled, "it's good of you, old fellow—really good of you! Business, my jolly old shipowner, waits for no man. Ali, my cheque-book!"

"A moment—just a moment, dear Mr. Bones," begged Fred. "You don't mind my calling you by the name which is already famous in the City?"

Bones looked dubious.

"Personally, I prefer Tibbetts," said Fred.

"Personally, dear old Fred, so do I," admitted Bones.

"I've come on a curious errand," said Fred in such hollow tones that Bones started. "The fact is, old man, I'm——"

He hung his head, and Bones laid a sympathetic hand on his shoulder.

"Anybody is liable to get that way, my jolly old roysterer," he said. "Speakin' for myself, drink has no effect upon me—due to my jolly old nerves of iron an' all that sort of thing."

"I'm ashamed of myself," said Fred.

"Nothing to be ashamed of, my poor old toper," said Bones honestly in error. "Why, I remember once——"

"As a business man, Mr. Tibbetts," said Fred bravely, "can you forgive sentiment?"

"Sentiment! Why, you silly old josser, I'm all sentiment, dear old thing! Why, I simply cry myself to sleep over dear old Charles What's-his-name's books!"

"It's sentiment," said Fred brokenly. "I just can't—I simply can't part with those two ships I sold you."

"Hey?" said Bones.

"They were your uncle's, but they have an association for me and my brother which it would be—er—profane to mention. Mr. Tibbetts, let us cry off our bargain."

Bones sniffed and rubbed his nose.

"Business, dear old Fred," he said gently. "Bear up an' play the man, as dear old Francis Drake said when they stopped him playin' cricket. Business, old friend. I'd like to oblige you, but——"

He shook his head rapidly

Mr. Fred slowly produced his cheque-book and laid it on the desk with the sigh of one who was about to indite his last wishes.

"You shall not be the loser," he said, with a catch in his voice, for he was genuinely grieved. "I must pay for my weakness. What is five hundred pounds?"

"What is a thousand, if it comes to that, Freddy?" said Bones. "Gracious goodness, I shall be awfully disappointed if you back out—I shall be so vexed, really."

"Seven hundred and fifty?" asked Fred, with pleading in his eye.

"Make it a thousand, dear old Fred," said Bones; "I can't add up fifties."

So "in consideration" (as Fred wrote rapidly and Bones signed more rapidly) "of the sum of one thousand pounds (say £1,000), the contract as between &c., &c.," was cancelled, and Fred became again the practical man of affairs.

"Dear old Fred," said Bones, folding the cheque and sticking it in his pocket, "I'm goin' to own up—frankness is a vice with me—that I don't understand much about the shippin' business. But tell me, my jolly old merchant, why do fellers sell you ships in the mornin' an' buy 'em back in the afternoon?"

"Business, Mr. Tibbetts," said Fred, smiling, "just big business."

Bones sucked an inky finger.

"Dinky business for me, dear old thing," he said. "I've got a thousand from you an' a thousand from the other Johnny who sold me two ships. Bless my life an' soul——"

"The other fellow," said Fred faintly—"a fellow from the United Merchant Shippers?"

"That was the dear lad," said Bones.

"And has he cried off his bargain, too?"

"Positively!" said Bones. "A very, very nice, fellow. He told me I could call him Joe—jolly old Joe!"

"Jolly old Joe!" repeated Fred mechanically, as he left the office, and all the way home he was saying "Jolly old Joe!"

Chapter 2

Hidden Treasure

M rs. Staleyborn's first husband was a dreamy Fellow of a Learned University.

Her second husband had begun life at the bottom of the ladder as a three-card trickster, and by strict attention to business and the exercise of his natural genius, had attained to the proprietorship of a bucket-shop.

When Mrs. Staleyborn was Miss Clara Smith, she had been housekeeper to Professor Whitland, a biologist who discovered her indispensability, and was only vaguely aware of the social gulf which yawned between the youngest son of the late Lord Bortledyne and the only daughter of Albert Edward Smith, mechanic. To the Professor she was Miss *H. Sapiens*—an agreeable, featherless plantigrade biped of the genus *Homo*. She was also thoroughly domesticated and cooked like an angel, a nice woman who apparently never knew that her husband had a Christian name, for she called him "Mr. Whitland" to the day of his death.

The strain and embarrassment of the new relationship with her master were intensified by the arrival of a daughter, and doubled when that daughter came to a knowledgeable age. Marguerite Whitland had the inherent culture of her father and the grace and delicate beauty which had ever distinguished the women of the house of Bortledyne.

When the Professor died, Mrs. Whitland mourned him in all sincerity. She was also relieved. One-half of the burden which lay upon her had been lifted; the second half was wrestling with the binomial theorem at Cheltenham College.

She had been a widow twelve months when she met Mr. Cresta Morris, and, if the truth be told, Mr. Cresta Morris more fulfilled her conception as to what a gentleman should look like than had the Professor. Mr. Cresta Morris wore white collars and beautiful ties, had a large gold watch-chain over what the French call poetically a *gilet de fantasie*, but which he, in his own homely fashion, described as a "fancy weskit." He smoked large cigars, was bluff and hearty, spoke to the widow—he was staying at Harrogate at the time in a hydropathic establishment—in a language which she could understand. Dimly she began to realize that the Professor had hardly spoken to her at all.

Mr. Cresta Morris was one of those individuals who employed a vocabulary of a thousand words, with all of which Mrs. Whitland was well acquainted; he was also a man of means and possessions, he explained to her. She, giving confidence for confidence, told of the house at Cambridge, the furniture, the library, the annuity of three hundred pounds, earmarked for his daughter's education, but mistakenly left to his wife for that purpose, also the four thousand three hundred pounds invested in War Stock, which was wholly her own.

Mr. Cresta Morris became more agreeable than ever. In three months they were married, in six months the old house at Cambridge had been disposed of, the library dispersed, as much of the furniture as Mr. Morris regarded as old-fashioned sold, and the relict of Professor Whitland was installed in a house in Brockley.

It was a nice house—in many ways nicer than the rambling old building in Cambridge, from Mrs. Morris's point of view. And she was happy in a tolerable, comfortable kind of fashion, and though she was wholly ignorant as to the method by which her husband made his livelihood, she managed to get along very well without enlightenment.

Marguerite was brought back from Cheltenham to grace the new establishment and assist in its management. She shared none of her mother's illusions as to the character of Mr. Cresta Morris, as that gentleman explained to a very select audience one January night.

Mr. Morris and his two guests sat before a roaring fire in the dining-room, drinking hot brandies-and-waters. Mrs. Morris had gone to bed; Marguerite was washing up, for Mrs. Morris had the "servant's mind," which means that she could never keep a servant.

The sound of crashing plates had come to the dining-room and interrupted Mr. Morris at a most important point of his narrative. He jerked his head round.

"That's the girl," he said; "she's going to be a handful."

"Get her married," said Job Martin wisely.

He was a hatchet-faced man with a reputation for common-sense. He had another reputation which need not be particularized at the moment.

"Married?" scoffed Mr. Morris. "Not likely!"

He puffed at his cigar thoughtfully for a moment, then:

"She wouldn't come in to dinner—did you notice that? We are not good enough for her. She's fly! Fly ain't the word for it. We always find her nosing and sneaking around."

"Send her back to school," said the third guest.

He was a man of fifty-five, broad-shouldered, clean-shaven, who had literally played many parts, for he had been acting in a touring company when Morris first met him—Mr. Timothy Webber, a man not unknown to the Criminal Investigation Department.

"She might have been useful," Mr. Morris went on regretfully, "very useful indeed. She is as pretty as a picture, I'll give her that due. Now, suppose she——"

Webber shook his head.

"It's my way or no way," he said decidedly. "I've been a month studying this fellow, and I tell you I know him inside out."

"Have you been to see him?" asked the second man.

"Am I a fool?" replied the other roughly. "Of course I have not been to see him. But there are ways of finding out, aren't there? He is not the kind of lad that you can work with a woman, not if she's as pretty as paint."

"What do they call him?" asked Morris.

"Bones," said Webber, with a little grin. "At least, he has letters which start 'Dear Bones,' so I suppose that's his nickname. But he's got all the money in the world. He is full of silly ass schemes, and he's romantic."

"What's that to do with it?" asked Job Martin, and Webber turned with a despairing shrug to Morris.

"For a man who is supposed to have brains——" he said, but Morris stopped him with a gesture.

"I see the idea—that's enough."

He ruminated again, chewing at his cigar, then, with a shake of his head——

"I wish the girl was in it."

"Why?" asked Webber curiously.

"Because she's——" He hesitated. "I don't know what she knows about me. I can guess what she guesses. I'd like to get her into something like this, to—to——" He was at a loss for a word.

"Compromise?" suggested the more erudite Webber.

"That's the word. I'd like to have her like that!" He put his thumb down on the table in an expressive gesture.

Marguerite, standing outside, holding the door-handle hesitating as to whether she should carry in the spirit kettle which Mr. Morris had ordered, stood still and listened.

The houses in Oakleigh Grove were built in a hurry, and at best were not particularly sound-proof. She stood fully a quarter of an hour whilst the three men talked in low tones, and any doubts she might have had as to the nature of her step-father's business were dispelled.

Again there began within her the old fight between her loyalty to her mother and loyalty to herself and her own ideals. She had lived through purgatory these past twelve months, and again and again she had resolved to end it all, only to be held by pity for the helpless woman she would be deserting. She told herself a hundred times that her mother was satisfied in her placid way with the life she was living, and that her departure would be rather a relief than a cause for uneasiness. Now she hesitated no longer, and went back to the kitchen, took off the apron she was wearing, passed along the side-passage, up the stairs to her room, and began to pack her little bag.

Her mother was facing stark ruin. This man had drawn into his hands every penny she possessed, and was utilizing it for the furtherance of his own nefarious business. She had an idea—vague as yet, but later taking definite shape—that if she might not save her mother from the wreck which was inevitable, she might at least save something of her little fortune.

She had "nosed around" to such purpose that she had discovered her step-father was a man who for years had evaded the grip of an exasperated constabulary. Some day he would fall, and in his fall bring down her mother.

Mr. Cresta Morris absorbed in the elaboration of the great plan, was reminded, by the exhaustion of visible refreshment, that certain of his instructions had not been carried out.

"Wait a minute," he said. "I told that girl to bring in the kettle at half-past nine. I'll go out and get it. Her royal highness wouldn't lower herself by bringing it in, I suppose!"

He found the kettle on the kitchen table, but there was no sign of Marguerite. This was the culmination of a succession of "slights" which she had put on him, and in a rage he walked along the passage, and yelled up the stairs:

"Marguerite!"

There was no reply, and he raced up to her room. It was empty, but what was more significant, her dresses and the paraphernalia which usually ornamented her dressing-table had disappeared.

He came down a very thoughtful man.

"She's hopped," he said laconically. "I was always afraid of that."

It was fully an hour before he recovered sufficiently to bring his mind to a scheme of such fascinating possibilities that even his step-daughter's flight was momentarily forgotten

On the following morning Mr. Tibbetts received a visitor.

That gentleman who was, according to the information supplied by Mr. Webber, addressed in intimate correspondence as "Dear Bones," was sitting in his most gorgeous private office, wrestling with a letter to the eminent firm of Timmins and Timmins, yacht agents, on a matter of a luckless purchase of his.

"Dear Sirs Genentlemen" (ran the letter. Bones wrote as he thought, thought faster than he wrote, and never opened a dictionary save to decide a bet)—"I told you I have told you 100000 times that the yacht *Luana* I bought from your cleint (a nice cleint I must say!!!) is a frord fruad and a *swindel*. It is much two too big. 2000 pounds was a swindel outraygious!! Well I've got it got it now so theres theirs no use crying over split milk. But do like a golly old yaght-seller get red of it rid of it. Sell it to *anybody* even for a 1000 pounds. I must have been mad to buy it but he was such a plausuble chap. . ."

This and more he wrote and was writing, when the silvery bell announced a visitor. It rang many times before he realized that he had sent his factotum, Ali Mahomet, to the South Coast to recover from a sniffle—the after-effects of a violent cold—which had been particularly distressing to both. Four times the bell rang, and four times Bones raised his head and scowled at the door, muttering violent criticisms of a man who at that moment was eighty-five miles away.

Then he remembered, leapt up, sprinted to the door, flung it open with an annoyed:

"Come in! What the deuce are you standing out there for?"

Then he stared at his visitor, choked, went very red, choked again, and fixed his monocle.

"Come in, young miss, come in," he said gruffly. "Jolly old bell's out of order. Awfully sorry and all that sort of thing. Sit down, won't you?"

In the outer office there was no visible chair. The excellent Ali preferred sitting on the floor, and visitors were not encouraged.

"Come into my office," said Bones, "my private office."

The girl had taken him in with one comprehensive glance, and a little smile trembled on the corner of her lips as she followed the harassed financier into his "holy of holies."

"My little den," said Bones incoherently. "Sit down, jolly old— young miss. Take my chair—it's the best. Mind how you step over that telephone wire. Ah!"

She did catch her feet in the flex, and he sprang to her assistance.

"Upsy, daisy, dear old—young miss, I mean."

It was a breathless welcome. She herself was startled by the warmth of it; he, for his part, saw nothing but grey eyes and a perfect mouth, sensed nothing but a delicate fragrance of a godlike presence.

"I have come to see you——" she began.

"Jolly good of you," said Bones enthusiastically. "You've no idea how fearsomely lonely I get sometimes. I often say to people: 'Look me up, dear old thing, any time between ten and twelve or two and four; don't stand on ceremony——'"

"I've come to see you——" she began again.

"You're a kind young miss," murmured Bones, and she laughed.

"You're not used to having girls in this office, are you?"

"You're the first," said Bones, with a dramatic flourish, "that ever burst tiddly-um-te-um!"

To be mistaken for a welcome visitor—she was that, did she but guess it—added to her natural embarrassment.

"Well," she said desperately, "I've come for work."

He stared at her, refixing his monocle.

"You've come for work my dear old—my jolly old—young miss?"

"I've come for work," she nodded.

Bones's face was very grave.

"You've come for work." He thought a moment; then: "What work? Of course," he added in a flurry, "there's plenty of work to do! Believe me, you don't know the amount I get through in this sanctum—that's Latin for 'private office'—and the wretched old place is never tidy— never! I am seriously thinking"—he frowned—"yes, I am very seriously thinking of sacking the lady who does the dusting. Why, do you know, this morning——"

Her eyes were smiling now, and she was to Bones's unsophisticated eyes, and, indeed, to eyes sophisticated, superhumanly lovely.

"I haven't come for a dusting job," she laughed.

"Of course you haven't," said Bones in a panic. "My dear old lady—my precious—my young person, I should have said—of course you haven't! You've come for a job—you've come to work! Well, you shall have it! Start right away!"

She stared.

"What shall I do?" she asked.

"What would I like you to do?" said Bones slowly. "What about scheming, getting out ideas, using brains, initiative, bright——" He trailed off feebly as she shook her head.

"Do you want a secretary?" she asked, and Bones's enthusiasm rose to the squeaking point.

"The very thing! I advertised in this morning's *Times*. You saw the advertisement?"

"You are not telling the truth," she said, looking at him with eyes that danced. "I read all the advertisement columns in *The Times* this morning, and I am quite sure that you did not advertise."

"I meant to advertise," said Bones gently. "I had the idea last night; that's the very piece of paper I was writing the advertisement on."

He pointed to a sheet upon the pad.

"A secretary? The very thing! Let me think."

He supported his chin upon one hand, his elbow upon another.

"You will want paper, pens, and ink—we have all those," he said. "There is a large supply in that cupboard. Also india-rubber. I am not sure if we have any india-rubber, but that can be procured. And a ruler," he said, "for drawing straight lines and all that sort of thing."

"And a typewriter?" she suggested.

Bones smacked his forehead with unnecessary violence.

"A typewriter! I knew this office wanted something. I said to Ali yesterday: 'You silly old ass——'"

"Oh, you have a girl?" she said disappointedly.

"Ali," said Bones, "is the name of a native man person who is devoted to me, body and soul. He has been, so to speak, in the family for years," he explained.

"Oh, it's a man," she said.

Bones nodded.

"Ali. Spelt A-l-y; it's Arabic."

"A native?"

Bones nodded.

"Of course he will not be in your way," ha hastened to explain. "He is in Bournemouth just now. He had sniffles." he explained rapidly, "and then he used to go to sleep, and snore. I hate people who snore, don't you?"

She laughed again. This was the most amazing of all possible employers.

"Of course," Bones went on, "I snore a bit myself. All thinkers do—I mean all brainy people. Not being a jolly old snorer yourself——"

"Thank you," said the girl.

Other tenants or the satellites of other tenants who occupied the palatial buildings wherein the office of Bones was situated saw, some few minutes later, a bare-headed young man dashing down the stairs three at a time; met him, half an hour later, staggering up those same stairs handicapped by a fifty-pound typewriter in one hand, and a chair in the style of the late Louis Quinze in the other, and wondered at the urgency of his movements.

"I want to tell you," said the girl, "that I know very little about shorthand."

"Shorthand is quite unnecessary, my dear—my jolly old stenographer," said Bones firmly. "I object to shorthand on principle, and I shall always object to it. If people," he went on, "were intended to write shorthand, they would have been born without the alphabet. Another thing——"

"One moment, Mr. Tibbetts," she said. "I don't know a great deal about typewriting, either."

Bones beamed.

"There I can help you," he said. "Of course it isn't necessary that you should know anything about typewriting. But I can give you a few hints," he said. "This thing, when you jiggle it up and down, makes the thingummy-bob run along. Every time you hit one of these letters—— I'll show you. . . Now, suppose I am writing 'Dear Sir,' I start with a 'D.' Now, where's that jolly old 'D'?" He scowled at the keyboard, shook his head, and shrugged his shoulders. "I thought so," he said; "there ain't a 'D.' I had an idea that that wicked old——"

"Here's the 'D,'" she pointed out.

Bones spent a strenuous but wholly delightful morning and afternoon. He was half-way home to his chambers in Curzon Street before he realized that he had not fixed the rather important question of salary. He looked forward to another pleasant morning making good that lapse.

It was his habit to remain late at his office at least three nights a week, for Bones was absorbed in his new career.

"Schemes Ltd." was no meaningless title. Bones had schemes which embraced every field of industrial, philanthropic, and social activity. He had schemes for building houses, and schemes for planting rose trees along all the railway tracks. He had schemes for building motor-cars, for founding labour colonies, for harnessing the rise and fall of the tides, he had a scheme for building a theatre where the audience sat on a huge turn-table, and, at the close of one act, could be twisted round, with no inconvenience to themselves, to face a stage which has been set behind them. Piqued by a certain strike which had caused him a great deal of inconvenience, he was engaged one night working out a scheme for the provision of municipal taxicabs, and he was so absorbed in his wholly erroneous calculations that for some time he did not hear the angry voices raised outside the door of his private office.

Perhaps it was that that portion of his mind which had been left free to receive impressions was wholly occupied with a scheme—which appeared in no books or records—for raising the wages of his new secretary.

But presently the noise penetrated even to him, and he looked up with a touch of annoyance.

"At this hour of the night! . . . Goodness gracious. . . respectable building!"

His disjointed comments were interrupted by the sound of a scuffle, an oath, a crash against his door and a groan, and Bones sprang to the door and threw it open.

As he did so a man who was leaning against it fell in.

"Shut the door, quick!" he gasped, and Bones obeyed.

The visitor who had so rudely irrupted himself was a man of middle age, wearing a coarse pea-jacket and blue jersey of a seaman, his peaked hat covered with dust, as Bones perceived later, when the sound of scurrying footsteps had died away.

The man was gripping his left arm as if in pain, and a thin trickle of red was running down the back of his big hand.

"Sit down, my jolly old mariner," said Bones anxiously. "What's the matter with you? What's the trouble, dear old sea-dog?"

The man looked up at him with a grimace.

"They nearly got it, the swine!" he growled.

He rolled up his sleeve and, deftly tying a handkerchief around a red patch, chuckled:

"It is only a scratch," he said. "They've been after me for two days, Harry Weatherall and Jim Curtis. But right's right all the world over. I've suffered enough to get what I've got—starved on the high seas, and starved on Lomo Island. Is it likely that I'm going to let them share?"

Bones shook his head.

"You sit down, my dear old fellow," he said sympathetically.

The man thrust his hands laboriously into his inside pocket and pulled out a flat oilskin case. From this he extracted a folded and faded chart.

"I was coming up to see a gentleman in these buildings," he said, "a gentleman named Tibbetts."

Bones opened his mouth to speak, but stopped himself.

"Me and Jim Curtis and young Harry, we were together in the *Serpent Queen*—my name's Dibbs. That's where we got hold of the yarn about Lomo Island, though we didn't believe there was anything in it. But when this Dago died——"

"Which Dago?" asked Bones.

"The Dago that knew all about it," said Mr. Dibbs impatiently, "and we come to split up his kit in his mess-bag, I found this." He shook the oilskin case in Bones's face. "Well, the first thing I did, when I got to Sydney, was to desert, and I got a chap from Wellington to put up the money to hire a boat to take me to Lomo. We were wrecked on Lomo."

"So you got there?" said Bones sympathetically.

"Six weeks I was on Lomo. Ate nothing but crabs, drank nothing but rain-water. But the stuff was there all right, only"—he was very emphatic, was this simple old sea-dog—"it wasn't under the third tree, but the fourth tree. I got down to the first of the boxes, and it was as much as I could do to lift it out. I couldn't trust any of the Kanaka boys who were with me."

"Naturally," said Bones. "An' I'll bet they didn't trust you, the naughty old Kanakas."

"Look here," said Mr. Dibbs, and he pulled out of his pocket a handful of gold coins which bore busts of a foreign-looking lady and gentleman. "Spanish gold, that is," he said. "There was four thousand in the little box. I filled both my pockets, and took 'em back to Sydney when we were picked up. I didn't dare try in Australia. 'That gold will keep,' I says to myself. 'I'll get back to England and find a man who will put up the money for an expedition'—a gentleman, you understand?"

"I quite understand," said Bones, all a-quiver with excitement.

"And then I met Harry and Jim. They said they'd got somebody who would put the money up, an American fellow, Rockefeller. Have you ever heard of him?"

"I've heard of him," said Bones; "he's got a paraffin mine."

"It may be he has, it may be he hasn't," said Mr. Dibbs and rose. "Well, sir, I'm very much obliged to you for your kindness. If you'll direct me to Mr. Tibbetts's office——"

It was a dramatic moment.

"I am Mr. Tibbetts," said Bones simply.

Blank incredulity was on the face of Mr. Dibbs.

"You?" he said. "But I thought Mr. Tibbetts was an older gentleman?"

"Dear old treasure-finder," said Bones, "be assured I am Mr. Tibbetts. This is my office, and this is my desk. People think I am older because——" He smiled a little sadly, then: "Sit down!" he thundered. "Let us go into this."

He went into the matter, and the City clocks were booming one when he led his mariner friend into the street.

He was late at the office the next morning, because he was young and healthy and required nine hours of the deepest slumber that Morpheus kept in stock.

The grey-eyed girl was typing at a very respectable speed the notes Bones had given her the evening before. There was a telegram awaiting him, which he read with satisfaction. Then:

"Leave your work, my young typewriter," said Bones imperiously. "I have a matter of the greatest importance to discuss with you! See that all the doors are closed," he whispered; "lock 'em if necessary."

"I hardly think that's necessary," said the girl. "You see, if anybody came and found all the doors locked——"

"Idiot!" said Bones, very red.

"I beg your pardon," said the startled girl.

"I was speaking to me," said Bones rapidly. "This is a matter of the greatest confidence, my jolly old Marguerite "—he paused, shaking at his temerity, for it was only on the previous day that he had discovered her name—"a matter which requires tact and discretion, young Marguerite——"

"You needn't say it twice," she said.

"Well once," said Bones, brightening up. "That's a bargain—I'll call you Marguerite once a day. Now, dear old Marguerite, listen to this."

She listened with the greatest interest, jotting down the preliminary expenses. Purchase of steamer, five thousand pounds; provisioning of same, three thousand pounds, etc., etc. She even undertook to make a copy of the plan which Mr. Dibbs had given into his charge, and which Bones told her had not left him day nor night.

"I put it in my pyjama pocket when I went to bed," he explained unnecessarily, "and——" He began to pat himself all over, consternation in his face.

"And you left it in your pyjama pocket," said the girl quietly. "I'll telephone to your house for it."

"Phew!" said Bones. "It seems incredible. I must have been robbed."

"I don't think so," said the girl; "it is probably under your pillow. Do you keep your pyjamas under your pillow?"

"That," said Bones, "is a matter which I never discuss in public. I hate to disappoint you, dear old Marguerite——"

"I'm sorry," said the girl, with such a simulation of regret that Bones dissolved into a splutter of contrition.

A commissionaire and a taxicab brought the plan, which was discovered where the girl in her wisdom had suggested.

"I'm not so sure how much money I'm going to make out of this," said Bones off-handedly, after a thorough and searching examination of the project. "It is certain to be about three thousand pounds—it may be a million or two million. It'll be good for you, dear old stenographer."

She looked at him.

"I have decided," said Bones, playing with his paper-knife, "to allow you a commission of seven and a half per cent. on all profits. Seven and a half per cent. on two million is, roughly, fifty thousand pounds——"

She laughed her refusal.

"I like to be fair," said Bones.

"You like to be generous," she corrected him, "and because I am a girl, and pretty——"

"Oh, I say," protested Bones feebly—"oh, really you are not pretty at all. I am not influenced by your perfectly horrible young face, believe me, dear old Miss Marguerite. Now, I've a sense of fairness, a sense of justice——"

"Now, listen to me, Mr. Tibbetts." She swung her chair round to face him squarely. "I've got to tell you a little story."

Bones listened to that story with compressed lips and folded arms. He was neither shocked nor amazed, and the girl was surprised.

"Hold hard, young miss," he said soberly. "If this is a jolly old swindle, and if the naughty mariner——"

"His name is Webber, and he is an actor," she interrupted.

"And dooced well he acted," admitted Bones. "Well, if this is so, what about the other johnny who's putting up ten thousand to my fifteen thousand?"

This was a facer for the girl, and Bones glared his triumph.

"That is what the wicked old ship-sailer said. Showed me the money, an' I sent him straight off on the job. He said he'd got a Stock Exchange person named Morris——"

"Morris!" gasped the girl. "That is my step-father!"

Bones jumped up, a man inspired.

"The naughty old One, who married your sainted mother?" he gurgled. "My miss! My young an' jolly old Marguerite!"

He sat down at his desk, yanked open the drawer, and slapped down his cheque-book.

"Three thousand pounds," he babbled, writing rapidly. "You'd better keep it for her, dear old friend of Faust."

"But I don't understand," she said, bewildered.

"Telegram," said Bones briefly. "Read it."

She picked up the buff form and read. It was postmarked from Cowes, and ran:

"In accordance your telegraphed instructions, have sold your schooner-yacht to Mr. Dibbs, who paid cash. Did not give name of owner. Dibbs did not ask to see boat. All he wanted was receipt for money."

"They are calling this afternoon for my fifteen thousand," said Bones, cackling light-headedly. "Ring up jolly old Scotland Yard, and ask 'em to send me all the police they've got in stock!"

Chapter 3

Bones and the Wharfingers

I

THE KITE WHEELING INVISIBLE IN the blue heavens, the vulture appearing mysteriously from nowhere in the track of the staggering buck, possess qualities which are shared by certain favoured human beings. No newspaper announced the fact that there had arrived in the City of London a young man tremendously wealthy and as tremendously inexperienced.

There were no meetings of organized robber gangs, where masked men laid nefarious plans and plots, but the instinct which called the kite to his quarry and the carrion to the kill brought many strangers—who were equally strange to Bones and to one another—to the beautiful office which he had fitted for himself for the better furtherance of his business.

One day a respectable man brought to Mr. Tibbetts a plan of a warehouse. He came like a gale of wind, almost before Bones had digested the name on the card which announced his existence and identity.

His visitor was red-faced and big, and had need to use a handkerchief to mop his brow and neck at intervals of every few minutes. His geniality was overpowering.

Before the startled Bones could ask his business, he had put his hat upon one chair, hooked his umbrella on another, and was unrolling, with that professional tremblement of hand peculiar to all who unroll large stiff sheets of paper, a large coloured plan, a greater portion of which was taken up by the River Thames, as Bones saw at a glance.

He knew that blue stood for water, and, twisting his neck, he read "Thames." He therefore gathered that this was the plan of a property adjacent to the London river.

"You're a busy man; and I'm a busy man," said the stentorian man breathlessly. "I've just bought this property, and if it doesn't interest you I'll eat my hat! My motto is small profits and quick returns. Keep your money at work, and you won't have to. Do you see what I mean?"

"Dear old hurricane," said Bones feebly, "this is awfully interesting, and all that sort of thing, but would you be so kind as to explain why and where—why you came in in this perfectly informal manner? Against all the rules of my office, dear old thing, if you don't mind me snubbing you a bit. You are sure you aren't hurt?" he asked.

"Not a bit, not a bit!" bellowed the intruder. "Honest John, I am—John Staines. You have heard of me?"

"I have," said Bones, and the visitor was so surprised that he showed it.

"You have?" he said, not without a hint of incredulity.

"Yes," said Bones calmly. "Yes, I have just heard you say it, Honest John Staines. Any relation to John o' Gaunt?"

This made the visitor look up sharply.

"Ha, ha!" he said, his laugh lacking sincerity. "You're a bit of a joker, Mr. Tibbetts. Now, what do you say to this? This is Stivvins' Wharf and Warehouse. Came into the market on Saturday, and I bought it on Saturday. The only river frontage which is vacant between Greenwich and Gravesend. Stivvins, precious metal refiner, went broke in the War, as you may have heard. Now, I am a man of few words and admittedly a speculator. I bought this property for fifteen thousand pounds. Show me a profit of five thousand pounds and it's yours."

Before Bones could speak, he stopped him with a gesture.

"Let me tell you this: if you like to sit on that property for a month, you'll make a sheer profit of twenty thousand pounds. You can afford to do it—I can't. I tell you there isn't a vacant wharfage between Greenwich and Gravesend, and here you have a warehouse with thirty thousand feet of floor-space, derricks—derrick, named after the hangman of that name: I'll bet you didn't know that?—cranes, everything in—— Well, it's not in apple-pie order," he admitted, "but it won't take much to make it so. What do you say?"

Bones started violently.

"Excuse me, old speaker, I was thinking of something else. Do you mind saying that all over again?"

Honest John Staines swallowed something and repeated his proposition.

Bones shook his head violently.

"Nothing doing!" he said. "Wharves and ships—*no!*"

But Honest John was not the kind that accepts refusal without protest.

"What I'll do," said he confidentially, "is this: I'll leave the matter for twenty-four hours in your hands."

"No, go, my reliable old wharf-seller," said Bones. "I never go up the river under any possible circumstances—— By Jove, I've got an idea!"

He brought his knuckly fist down upon the unoffending desk, and Honest John watched hopefully.

"Now, if—yes, it's an idea!"

Bones seized paper, and his long-feathered quill squeaked violently.

"That's it—a thousand members at ten pounds a year, four hundred bedrooms at, say, ten shillings a night—— How many is four hundred times ten shillings multiplied by three hundred and sixty-five? Well, let's say twenty thousand pounds. That's it! A club!"

"A club?" said Honest John blankly.

"A river club. You said Greenhithe—that's somewhere near Henley, isn't it?"

Honest John sighed.

"No, sir," he said gently, "it's in the other direction—toward the sea."

Bones dropped his pen and pinched his lip in an effort of memory.

"Is it? Now, where was I thinking about? I know—Maidenhead! Is it near Maidenhead?"

"It's in the opposite direction from London," said the perspiring Mr. Staines.

"Oh!"

Bones's interest evaporated.

"No good to me, my old speculator. Wharves! Bah!"

He shook his head violently, and Mr. Staines aroused himself.

"I'll tell you what I'll do, Mr. Tibbetts," he said simply; "I'll leave the plans with you. I'm going down into the country for a night. Think it over. I'll call to-morrow afternoon."

Bones still shook his head.

"No go, nothin' doin'. Finish this palaver, dear old Honesty!"

"Anyway, no harm is done," urged Mr. Staines. "I ask you, is there any harm done? You have the option for twenty-four hours. I'll roll the plans up so that they won't be in the way. Good morning!"

He was out of the office door before Bones could as much as deliver the preamble to the stern refusal he was preparing.

At three o'clock that afternoon came two visitors. They sent in a card bearing the name of a very important Woking firm of land agents, and they themselves were not without dignity of bearing.

There was a stout gentleman and a thin gentleman, and they tiptoed into the presence of Bones with a hint of reverence which was not displeasing.

"We have come on a rather important matter," said the thin gentleman. "We understand you have this day purchased Stivvins' Wharf——"

"Staines had no right to sell it?" burst in the stout man explosively. "A dirty mean trick, after all that he promised us! It is just his way of getting revenge, selling the property to a stranger!"

"Mr. Sole"—the thin gentleman's voice and attitude were eloquent of reproof—"*please* restrain yourself! My partner is annoyed," he explained "and not without reason. We offered fifty thousand pounds for Stivvins', and Staines, in sheer malice, has sold the property—which is virtually necessary to our client—literally behind our backs. Now, Mr. Tibbetts, are you prepared to make a little profit and transfer the property to us?"

"But——" began Bones.

"We will give you sixty thousand," said the explosive man. "Take it or leave it—sixty thousand."

"But, my dear old Boniface," protested Bones, "I haven't bought the property—really and truly I haven't. Jolly old Staines wanted me to buy it, but I assure you I didn't."

The stout man looked at him with glazed eyes, pulled himself together, and suggested huskily:

"Perhaps you will buy it—at his price—and transfer it to us?"

"But why? Nothing to do with me, my old estate agent and auctioneer. Buy it yourself. Good afternoon. *Good* afternoon!"

He ushered them out in a cloud of genial commonplaces.

In the street they looked at one another, and then beckoned Mr. Staines, who was waiting on the other side of the road.

"This fellow is either as wide as Broad Street or he's a babe in arms," said the explosive man huskily.

"Didn't he fall?" asked the anxious Staines.

"Not noticeably," said the thin man. "This is your scheme, Jack, and if I've dropped four thousand over that wharf, there's going to be trouble."

Mr. Staines looked very serious.

"Give him the day," he begged. "I'll try him to-morrow—I haven't lost faith in that lad."

As for Bones, he made an entry in his secret ledger.

"A person called Stains and two perrsons called Sole Bros. Brothers tryed me with the old Fiddle Trick. You take a Fiddel in a Pawn

Brokers leave it with him along comes another Felow and pretends its a Stadivarious Stradivarious a valuable Fiddel. 2nd Felow offers to pay fablous sum pawnbroker says I'll see. When 1st felow comes for his fiddel pawnbroker buys it at fablous sum to sell it to the 2nd felow. But 2nd felow doesn't turn up.

"*Note.*—1st Felow called himself Honest John!! I dout if I dought it."

Bones finished his entries, locked away his ledger, and crossed the floor to the door of the outer office.

He knocked respectfully, and a voice bade him come in.

It is not usual for the principal of a business to knock respectfully or otherwise on the door of the outer office, but then it is not usual for an outer office to house a secretary of such transcendental qualities, virtue, and beauty as were contained in the person of Miss Marguerite Whitland.

The girl half turned to the door and flashed a smile which was of welcome and reproof.

"Please, Mr. Tibbetts," she pleaded, "do not knock at my door. Don't you realize that it isn't done?"

"Dear old Marguerite," said Bones solemnly, "a new era has dawned in the City. As jolly old Confusicus says: 'The moving finger writes, and that's all about it.' Will you deign to honour me with your presence in my sanctorum, and may I again beg of you"—he leant his bony knuckles on the ornate desk which he had provided for her, and looked down upon her soberly—"may I again ask you, dear old miss, to let me change offices? It's a little thing, dear old miss. I'm never, never goin' to ask you to dinner again, but this is another matter. I am out of my element in such a place as——" He waved his hand disparagingly towards his sanctum. "I'm a rough old adventurer, used to sleeping in the snow—hardships—I can sleep anywhere."

"Anyway, you're not supposed to sleep in the office," smiled the girl, rising.

Bones pushed open the door for her, bowed as she passed, and followed her. He drew a chair up to the desk, and she sat down without further protest, because she had come to know that his attentions, his extravagant politeness and violent courtesies, signified no more than was apparent—namely, that he was a great cavalier at heart.

"I think you ought to know," he said gravely, "that an attempt was made this morning to rob me of umpteen pounds."

"To rob you?" said the startled girl.

"To rob me," said Bones, with relish. "A dastardly plot, happily frustrated by the ingenuity of the intended victim. I don't want to boast, dear old miss. Nothing is farther from my thoughts or wishes, but what's more natural when a fellow is offered a——"

He stopped and frowned.

"Yes?"

"A precious metal refiner's—— That's rum," said Bones.

"Rum?" repeated the girl hazily. "What is rum?"

"Of all the rummy old coincidences," said Bones, with restrained and hollow enthusiasm—"why, only this morning I was reading in *Twiddly Bits*, a ripping little paper, dear old miss—— There's a column called 'Things You Ought to Know,' which is honestly worth the twopence."

"I know it," said the girl curiously. "But what did you read?"

"It was an article called 'Fortunes Made in Old Iron,'" said Bones. "Now, suppose this naughty old refiner—— By Jove, it's an idea!"

He paced the room energetically, changing the aspect of his face with great rapidity, as wandering thoughts crowded in upon him and vast possibilities shook their alluring banners upon the pleasant scene he conjured. Suddenly he pulled himself together, shot out his cuffs, opened and closed all the drawers of his desk as though seeking something—he found it where he had left it, hanging on a peg behind the door, and put it on—and said with great determination and briskness:

"Stivvins' Wharf, Greenhithe. You will accompany me. Bring your note-book. It is not necessary to bring a typewriter. I will arrange for a taxicab. We can do the journey in two hours."

"But where are you going?" asked the startled girl.

"To Stivvins'. I am going to look at this place. There is a possibility that certain things have been overlooked. Never lose an opportunity, dear old miss. We magnates make our fortune by never ignoring the little things."

But still she demurred, being a very sane, intelligent girl, with an imagination which produced no more alluring mental picture than a cold and draughty drive, a colder and draughtier and even more depressing inspection of a ruined factory, and such small matters as a lost lunch.

But Bones was out of the room, in the street, had flung himself upon a hesitant taxi-driver, had bullied and cajoled him to take a monstrous and undreamt-of journey for a man who, by his own admission, had only sufficient petrol to get his taxi home, and when the girl came down she found Bones, with his arm entwined through the open window of the door, giving explicit instructions as to the point on the river where Stivvins' Wharf was to be found.

II

BONES RETURNED TO HIS OFFICE alone. The hour was six-thirty, and he was a very quiet and thoughtful young man. He almost tiptoed into his office, closed and locked the door behind him, and sat at his desk with his head in his hands for the greater part of half an hour.

Then he unrolled the plan of the wharf, hoping that his memory had not played him false. Happily it had not. On the bottom right-hand corner Mr. Staines had written his address! "Stamford Hotel, Blackfriars."

Bones pulled a telegraph form from his stationery rack and indited an urgent wire.

Mr. Staines, at the moment of receiving that telegram, was sitting at a small round table in the bar of The Stamford, listening in silence to certain opinions which were being expressed by his two companions in arms and partners in misfortune, the same opinions relating in a most disparaging manner to the genius, the foresight, and the constructive ability of one who in his exuberant moments described himself as Honest John.

The explosive gentleman had just concluded a fanciful picture of what would happen to Honest John if he came into competition with the average Bermondsey child of tender years.

Honest John took the telegram and opened it. He read it and gasped. He stood up and walked to the light, and read it again, then returned, his eyes shining, his face slightly flushed.

"You're clever, ain't you?" he asked. "You're wise—I don't think! Look at this!"

He handed the telegram to the nearest of his companions, who was the tall, thin, and non-explosive partner, and he in turn passed it without a word to his more choleric companion.

"You don't mean to say he's going to buy it?"

"That's what it says, doesn't it?" said the triumphant Mr. Staines.

"It's a catch," said the explosive man suspiciously.

"Not on your life," replied the scornful Staines. "Where does the catch come in? We've done nothing he could catch us for?"

"Let's have a look at that telegram again," said the thin man, and, having read it in a dazed way, remarked: "He'll wait for you at the office until nine. Well, Jack, nip up and fix that deal. Take the transfers with you. Close it and take his cheque. Take anything he'll give you, and get a special clearance in the morning, and, anyway, the business is straight."

Honest John breathed heavily through his nose and staggered from the bar, and the suspicious glances of the barman were, for once, unjustified, for Mr. Staines was labouring under acute emotions.

He found Bones sitting at his desk, a very silent, taciturn Bones, who greeted him with a nod.

"Sit down," said Bones. "I'll take that property. Here's my cheque."

With trembling fingers Mr. Staines prepared the transfers. It was he who scoured the office corridors to discover two agitated char-ladies who were prepared to witness his signature for a consideration.

He folded the cheque for twenty thousand pounds reverently and put it into his pocket, and was back again at the Stamford Hotel so quickly that his companions could not believe their eyes.

"Well, this is the rummiest go I have ever known," said the explosive man profoundly. "You don't think he expects us to call in the morning and buy it back, do you?"

Staines shook his head.

"I know he doesn't," he said grimly. "In fact, he as good as told me that that business of buying a property back was a fake."

The thin man whistled.

"The devil he did! Then what made him buy it?"

"He's been there. He mentioned he had seen the property," said Staines. And then, as an idea occurred to them all simultaneously, they looked at one another.

The stout Mr. Sole pulled a big watch from his pocket.

"There's a caretaker at Stivvins', isn't there?" he said. "Let's go down and see what has happened."

Stivvins' Wharf was difficult of approach by night. It lay off the main Woolwich Road, at the back of another block of factories, and to reach its dilapidated entrance gates involved an adventurous march through a number of miniature shell craters. Night, however, was merciful in that it hid the desolation which is called Stivvins' from the fastidious eye of man. Mr. Sole, who was not aesthetic and by no means poetical, admitted that Stivvins' gave him the hump.

It was ten o'clock by the time they had reached the wharf, and half-past ten before their hammering on the gate aroused the attention of the night-watchman—who was also the day-watchman—who occupied what had been in former days the weigh-house, which he had converted into a weatherproof lodging.

"Hullo!" he said huskily. "I was asleep."

He recognized Mr. Sole, and led the way to his little bunk-house.

"Look here, Tester," said Sole, who had appointed the man, "did a young swell come down here to-day?"

"He did," said Mr. Tester, "and a young lady. They gave Mr. Staines's name, and asked to be showed round, and," he added, "I showed 'em round."

"Well, what happened?" asked Staines.

"Well," said the man, "I took 'em in the factory, in the big building, and then this young fellow asked to see the place where the metal was kept."

"What metal?" asked three voices at one and the same time.

"That's what I asked," said Mr. Tester, with satisfaction. "I told 'em Stivvins dealt with all kinds of metal, so the gent says: 'What about gold?'"

"What about gold?" repeated Mr. Staines thoughtfully. "And what did you say?"

"Well, as a matter of fact," explained Tester, "I happen to know this place, living in the neighbourhood, and I used to work here about eight years ago, so I took 'em down to the vault."

"To the vault?" said Mr. Staines. "I didn't know there was a vault."

"It's under the main office. You must have seen the place," said Tester. "There's a big steel door with a key in it—at least, there was a key in it, but this young fellow took it away with him."

Staines gripped his nearest companion in sin, and demanded huskily:

"Did they find anything in—in the vault?"

"Blessed if I know!" said the cheerful Tester, never dreaming that he was falling very short of the faith which at that moment, and only at that moment, had been reposed in him. "They just went in. I've never been inside the place myself."

"And you stood outside, like a—a——"

"Blinking image!" said the explosive companion.

"You stood outside like a blinking image, and didn't attempt to go in, and see what they were looking at?" said Mr. Staines heatedly. "How long were they there?"

"About ten minutes."

"And then they came out?"

Tester nodded.

"Did they bring anything out with them?"

"Nothing," said Mr. Tester emphatically.

"Did this fellow—what's his name?—look surprised or upset?" persisted the cross-examining Honest John.

"He was a bit upset, now you come to mention it, agitated like, yes," said Tester, reviewing the circumstances in a new light. "His 'and was, so to speak, shaking."

"Merciful Moses!" This pious ejaculation was from Mr. Staines. "He took away the key, you say. And what are you supposed to be here for?" asked Mr. Staines violently. "You allow this fellow to come and take our property away. Where is the place?"

Tester led the way across the littered yard, explaining en route that he was fed up, and why he was fed up, and what they could do to fill the vacancy which would undoubtedly occur the next day, and where they could go to, so far as he was concerned, and so, unlocking one rusty lock after another, passed through dark and desolate offices, full of squeaks and scampers, down a short flight of stone steps to a most uncompromising steel door at which they could only gaze.

III

BONES WAS AT HIS OFFICE early the following rooming, but he was not earlier than Mr. Staines, who literally followed him into his office and slammed down a slip of paper under his astonished and gloomy eye.

"Hey, hey, what's this?" said Bones irritably. "What the dooce is this, my wicked old fiddle fellow?"

"Your cheque," said Mr. Staines firmly. "And I'll trouble you for the key of our strong-room."

"The key of your strong-room?" repeated Bones. "Didn't I buy this property?"

"You did and you didn't. To cut a long story short, Mr. Tibbetts, I have decided not to sell—in fact, I find that I have done an illegal thing in selling at all."

Bones shrugged his shoulders. Remember that he had slept, or half-slept, for some nine hours, and possibly his views had undergone a change. What he would have done is problematical, because at that moment the radiant Miss Whitland passed into her office, and Bones's acute ear heard the snap of her door.

"One moment," he said gruffly, "one moment, old Honesty."

He strode through the door which separated the private from the public portion of his suite, and Mr. Staines listened. He listened at varying distances from the door, and in his last position it would have required the most delicate of scientific instruments to measure the distance between his ear and the keyhole. He heard nothing save the wail of a Bones distraught, and the firm "No's" of a self-possessed female.

Then, after a heart-breaking silence Bones strode out, and Mr. Staines did a rapid sprint, so that he might be found standing in an attitude of indifference and thought near the desk. The lips of Bones were tight and compressed. He opened the drawer, pulled out the transfers, tossed them across to Mr. Staines.

"Key," said Bones, chucking it down after the document.

He picked up his cheque and tore it into twenty pieces.

"That's all," said Bones, and Mr. Staines beat a tremulous retreat.

When the man had gone, Bones returned to the girl who was sitting at her table before her typewriter. It was observable that her lips were compressed too.

"Young Miss Whitland," said Bones, and his voice was hoarser than ever, "never, never in my life will I ever forgive myself!"

"Oh, please, Mr. Tibbetts," said the girl a little wearily, "haven't I told you that I have forgiven you? And I am sure you had no horrid thought in your mind, and that you just acted impulsively."

Bones bowed his head, at once a sign of agreement and a crushed spirit.

"The fact remains, dear old miss," he said brokenly, "that I did kiss you in that beastly old private vault. I don't know what made me do it," he gulped, "but I did it. Believe me, young miss, that spot was sacred. I wanted to buy the building to preserve it for all time, so that no naughty old foot should tread upon that hallowed ground. You think that's nonsense!"

"Mr. Tibbetts."

"Nonsense, I say, romantic and all that sort of rot." Bones threw out his arms. "I must agree with you. But, believe me, Stivvins' Wharf is hallowed ground, and I deeply regret that you would not let me buy it and turn it over to the jolly old Public Trustee or one of those johnnies. . . You do forgive me?"

She laughed up in his face, and then Bones laughed, and they laughed together.

Chapter 4

The Plover Light Car

The door of the private office opened and after a moment closed. It was, in fact, the private door of the private office, reserved exclusively for the use of the Managing Director of Schemes Limited. Nevertheless, a certain person had been granted the privilege of ingress and egress through that sacred portal, and Mr. Tibbetts, yclept Bones, crouching over his desk, the ferocity of his countenance intensified by the monocle which was screwed into his eye, and the terrific importance of his correspondence revealed by his disordered hair and the red tongue that followed the movements of his pen, did not look up.

"Put it down, put it down, young miss," he murmured, "on the table, on the floor, anywhere."

There was no answer, and suddenly Bones paused and scowled at the half-written sheet before him.

"That doesn't look right." He shook his head. "I don't know what's coming over me. Do you spell 'cynical' with one 'k' or two?"

Bones looked up.

He saw a brown-faced man, with laughing grey eyes, a tall man in a long overcoat, carrying a grey silk hat in his hand.

"Pardon me, my jolly old intruder," said Bones with dignity, "this is a private——" Then his jaw dropped and he leant on the desk for support. "Not my—— Good heavens!" he squeaked, and then leapt across the room, carrying with him the flex of his table lamp, which fell crashing to the floor.

"Ham, you poisonous old reptile!" He seized the other's hand in his bony paw, prancing up and down, muttering incoherently.

"Sit down, my jolly old Captain. Let me take your overcoat. Well! Well! Well! Give me your hat, dear old thing—dear old Captain, I mean. This is simply wonderful! This is one of the most amazin' experiences I've ever had, my dear old sportsman and officer. How long have you been home? How did you leave the Territory? Good heavens! We must have a bottle on this!"

"Sit down, you noisy devil," said Hamilton, pushing his erstwhile subordinate into a chair, and pulling up another to face him.

"So this is your boudoir!" He glanced round admiringly. "It looks rather like the waiting-room of a *couturière*."

"My dear old thing," said the shocked Bones, "I beg you, if you please, remember, remember——" He lowered his voice, and the last word was in a hoarse whisper, accompanied by many winks, nods, and pointings at and to a door which led from the inner office apparently to the outer. "There's a person, dear old man of the world—a young person—well brought up——"

"What the——" began Hamilton.

"Don't be peeved!" Bones's knowledge of French was of the haziest. "Remember, dear old thing," he said solemnly, wagging his inky forefinger, "as an employer of labour, I must protect the young an' innocent, my jolly old skipper."

Hamilton looked round for a missile, and could find nothing better than a crystal paper-weight, which looked too valuable to risk.

"'*Couturière*,'" he said acidly, "is French for 'dressmaker.'"

"French," said Bones, "is a language which I have always carefully avoided. I will say no more—you mean well, Ham."

Thereafter followed a volley of inquiries, punctuated at intervals by genial ceremony, for Bones would rise from his chair, walk solemnly round the desk, and as solemnly shake hands with his former superior.

"Now, Bones," said Hamilton at last, "will you tell me what you are doing?"

Bones shrugged his shoulders.

"Business," he said briefly. "A deal now and again, dear old officer. Make a thousand or so one week, lose a hundred or so the next."

"But what are you doing?" persisted Hamilton.

Again Bones shrugged, but with more emphasis.

"I suppose," he confessed, with a show of self-deprecation which his smugness belied, "I suppose I am one of those jolly old spiders who sit in the centre of my web, or one of those perfectly dinky little tigers who sit in my jolly old lair, waiting for victims.

"Of course, it's cruel sport"—he shrugged again, toying with his ivory paper-knife—"but one must live. In the City one preys upon other ones."

"Do the other ones do any preying at all?" asked Hamilton.

Up went Bones's eyebrows.

"They try," he said tersely, and with compressed lips. "Last week a fellow tried to sell me his gramophone, but I had a look at it. As I suspected, it had no needle. A gramophone without a needle," said Bones, "as you probably know, my dear old musical one, is wholly useless."

"But you can buy them at a bob a box," said Hamilton.

Bones's face fell.

"Can you really?" he demanded. "You are not pulling my leg, or anything? That's what the other fellow said. I do a little gambling," Bones went on, "not on the Stock Exchange or on the race-course, you understand, but in Exchanges."

"Money Exchanges?"

Bones bowed his head.

"For example," he said, "to-day a pound is worth thirty-two francs, to-morrow it is worth thirty-four francs. To-day a pound is worth four dollars seventy-seven——"

"As a matter of fact, it is three dollars ninety-seven," interrupted Hamilton.

"Ninety-seven or seventy-seven," said Bones irritably, "what is four shillings to men like you or me, Hamilton? We can well afford it."

"My dear chap," said Hamilton, pardonably annoyed, "there is a difference of four shillings between your estimate and the rate."

"What is four shillings to you or me?" asked Bones again, shaking his head solemnly. "My dear old Ham, don't be mean."

There was a discreet tap on the door, and Bones rose with every evidence of agitation.

"Don't stir, dear old thing," he pleaded in a husky whisper. "Pretend not to notice, dear old Ham. Don't be nervous—wonderful young lady——"

Then, clearing his throat noisily, "Come in!" he roared in the tone that a hungry lion might have applied to one of the early Christian martyrs who was knocking by mistake on the door of his den.

In spite of all injunctions, Hamilton did look, and he did stare, and he did take a great deal of notice, for the girl who came in was well worth looking at. He judged her to be about the age of twenty-one. "Pretty" would be too feeble a word to employ in describing her. The russet-brown hair, dressed low over her forehead, emphasized the loveliness of eyes set wide apart and holding in their clear depths all the magic and mystery of womanhood.

She was dressed neatly. He observed, too, that she had an open book under her arm and a pencil in her hand, and it dawned upon him slowly that this radiant creature was—Bones's secretary!

Bones's secretary!

He stared at Bones, and that young man, very red in the face, avoided his eye.

Bones was standing by the desk, in the attitude of an after-dinner speaker who was stuck for the right word. In moments of extreme agitation Bones's voice became either a growl or a squeak—the bottom register was now in exercise.

"Did—did you want me, young miss?" he demanded gruffly.

The girl at the door hesitated.

"I'm sorry—I didn't know you were engaged. I wanted to see you about the Abyssinian——"

"Come in, come in, certainly," said Bones more gruffly than ever. "A new complication, young miss?"

She laid a paper on the desk, taking no more notice of Hamilton than if he were an ornament on the chimney-piece.

"The first instalment of the purchase price is due to-day," she said.

"Is it?" said Bones, with his extravagant surprise. "Are you certain, young miss? This day of all days—and it's a Thursday, too," he added unnecessarily.

The girl smiled and curled her lip, but only for a second.

"Well, well," said Bones, "it's a matter of serious importance. The cheque, jolly old young miss, we will sign it and you will send it off. Make it out for the full amount——"

"For the three thousand pounds?" said the girl.

"For the three thousand pounds," repeated Bones soberly. He put in his monocle and glared at her. "For the three thousand pounds," he repeated.

She stood waiting, and Bones stood waiting, he in some embarrassment as to the method by which the interview might be terminated and his secretary dismissed without any wound to her feelings.

"Don't you think to-morrow would do for the cheque?" she asked.

"Certainly, certainly," said Bones. "Why not? To-morrow's Friday, ain't it?"

She inclined her head and walked out of the room, and Bones cleared his throat once more.

"Bones——"

The young man turned to meet Hamilton's accusing eye.

"Bones," said Hamilton gently, "who is the lady?"

"Who is the lady?" repeated Bones, with a cough. "The lady is my secretary, dear old inquisitor."

"So I gather," said Hamilton.

"She is my secretary," repeated Bones. "An extremely sensible young woman, extremely sensible."

"Don't be silly," said Hamilton. "Plenty of people are sensible. When you talk about sensible young women, you mean plain young women."

"That's true," said Bones; "I never thought of that. What a naughty old mind you have, Ham."

He seemed inclined to change the subject.

"And now, dear old son," said Bones, with a brisk return to his what-can-I-do-for-you air, "to business! You've come, dear old thing, to consult me."

"You're surprisingly right," said Hamilton.

"Well," said Bones, trying three drawers of his desk before he could find one that opened, "have a cigar, and let us talk."

Hamilton took the proffered weed and eyed it suspiciously.

"Is this one that was given to you, or one that you bought?" he demanded.

"That, my jolly old officer," said Bones, "is part of a job lot that I bought pretty cheap. I've got a rare nose for a bargain——"

"Have you a rare nose for a cigar, that's the point?" asked Hamilton, as he cut off the end and lit it gingerly.

"Would I give you a bad cigar?" asked the indignant Bones. "A gallant old returned warrior, comrade of my youth, and all that sort of thing! My dear old Ham!"

"I'll tell you in a minute," said Hamilton, and took two draws.

Bones, who was no cigar smoker, watched the proceedings anxiously. Hamilton put the cigar down very gently on the corner of the desk.

"Do you mind if I finish this when nobody's looking?" he asked.

"Isn't it all right?" asked Bones. "Gracious heavens! I paid fifty shillings a hundred for those! Don't say I've been done."

"I don't see how you could be done at that price," said Hamilton, and brushed the cigar gently into the fireplace. "Yes, I have come to consult you, Bones," he went on. "Do you remember some eight months ago I wrote to you telling you that I had been offered shares in a motor-car company?"

Bones had a dim recollection that something of the sort had occurred, and nodded gravely.

"It seemed a pretty good offer to me," said Hamilton reflectively. "You remember I told you there was a managership attached to the holding of the shares?"

Bones shifted uneasily in his chair, sensing a reproach.

"My dear old fellow——" he began feebly.

"Wait a bit," said Hamilton. "I wrote to you and asked you your advice. You wrote back, telling me to have nothing whatever to do with the Plover Light Car Company."

"Did I?" said Bones. "Well, my impression was that I advised you to get into it as quickly as you possibly could. Have you my letter, dear old thing?"

"I haven't," said Hamilton.

"Ah," said Bones triumphantly, "there you are! You jolly old rascal, you are accusing me of putting you off——"

"Will you wait, you talkative devil?" said Hamilton. "I pointed out to you that the prospects were very alluring. The Company was floated with a small capital——"

Again Bones interrupted, and this time by rising and walking solemnly round the table to shake hands with him.

"Hamilton, dear old skipper," he pleaded. "I was a very busy man at that time. I admit I made a mistake, and possibly diddled you out of a fortune. But my intention was to write to you and tell you to get into it, and how I ever came to tell you *not* to get into it—well, my poor old speculator, I haven't the slightest idea!"

"The Company——" began Hamilton.

"I know, I know," said Bones, shaking his head sadly and fixing his monocle—a proceeding rendered all the more difficult by the fact that his hand never quite overtook his face. "It was an error on my part, dear old thing. I know the Company well. Makes a huge profit! You can see the car all over the town. I think the jolly old Partridge——"

"Plover," said Hamilton.

"Plover, I mean. They've got another kind of car called the Partridge," explained Bones. "Why, it's one of the best in the market. I thought of buying one myself. And to think that I put you off that Company! Tut, tut! Anyway, dear old man," he said, brightening up, "most of the good fish is in the sea, and it only goes bad when it comes out of the sea. Have you ever noticed that, my dear old naturalist?"

"Wait a moment. Will you be quiet?" said the weary Hamilton. "I'm trying to tell you my experiences. I put the money—four thousand pounds—into this infernal Company.

"Eh?"

"I put the money into the Company, I tell you, against your advice. The Company is more or less a swindle."

Bones sat down slowly in his chair and assumed his most solemn and business-like face.

"Of course, it keeps within the law, but it's a swindle, none the less. They've got a wretched broken-down factory somewhere in the North, and the only Plover car that's ever been built was made by a Scottish contractor at a cost of about twice the amount which the Company people said that they would charge for it."

"What did I say?" said Bones quietly. "Poor old soul, I do not give advice without considering matters, especially to my dearest friend. A company like this is obviously a swindle. You can tell by the appearance of the cars——"

"There was only one car ever made," interrupted Hamilton.

"I should have said car," said the unperturbed Bones. "The very appearance of it shows you that the thing is a swindle from beginning to end. Oh, why did you go against my advice, dear old Ham? Why did you?"

"You humbug!" said the wrathful Hamilton. "You were just this minute apologising for giving me advice."

"That," said Bones cheerfully, "was before I'd heard your story. Yes, Ham, you've been swindled." He thought a moment. "Four thousand pounds!"

And his jaw dropped.

Bones had been dealing in large sums of late, and had forgotten just the significance of four thousand pounds to a young officer. He was too much of a little gentleman to put his thoughts into words, but it came upon him like a flash that the money which Hamilton had invested in the Plover Light Car Company was every penny he possessed in the world, a little legacy he had received just before Bones had left the Coast, plus all his savings for years.

"Ham," he said hollowly, "I am a jolly old rotter! Here I've been bluffing and swanking to you when I ought to have been thinking out a way of getting things right."

Hamilton laughed.

"I'm afraid you're not going to get things right, Bones," he said. "The only thing I did think was that you might possibly know something about this firm."

At any other moment Bones would have claimed an extensive acquaintance with the firm and its working, but now he shook his head, and Hamilton sighed.

"Sanders told me to come up and see you," he said. "Sanders has great faith in you, Bones."

Bones went very red, coughed, picked up his long-plumed pen and put it down again.

"At any rate," said Hamilton, "you know enough about the City to tell me this—is there any chance of my getting this money back?"

Bones rose jerkily.

"Ham," he said, and Hamilton sensed a tremendous sincerity in his voice, "that money's going to come back to you, or the name of Augustus Tibbetts goes down in the jolly old records as a failure."

A minute later Captain Hamilton found himself hand-shook from the room. Here for Bones was a great occasion. With both elbows on the desk, and two hands searching his hair, he sat worrying out what he afterwards admitted was the most difficult problem that ever confronted him.

After half an hour's hair-pulling he went slowly across his beautiful room and knocked discreetly on the door of the outer office.

Miss Marguerite Whitland had long since grown weary of begging him to drop this practice. She found it a simple matter to say "Come in!" and Bones entered, closing the door behind him, and stood in a deferential attitude two paces from the closed door.

"Young miss," he said quietly, "may I consult you?"

"You may even consult me," she said as gravely.

"It is a very curious problem, dear old Marguerite," said Bones in a low, hushed tone. "It concerns the future of my very dearest friend— the very dearest friend in all the world," he said emphatically, "of the male sex," he added hastily. "Of course, friendships between jolly old officers are on a different plane, if you understand me, to friendships between—I mean to say, dear old thing, I'm not being personal or drawing comparisons, because the feeling I have for you——"

Here his eloquence ran dry. She knew him now well enough to be neither confused nor annoyed nor alarmed when Bones broke forth into an exposition of his private feelings. Very calmly she returned the conversation to the rails.

"It is a matter which concerns a very dear friend of yours," she said suggestively, and Bones nodded and beamed.

"Of course you guessed that," he said admiringly. "You're the jolliest old typewriter that ever lived! I don't suppose any other young woman in London would have——"

"Oh, yes, they would," she said. "You'd already told me. I suppose that you've forgotten it."

"Well, to cut a long story short, dear old Miss Marguerite," said Bones, leaning confidentially on the table and talking down into her upturned lace, "I must find the whereabouts of a certain rascal or rascals, trading or masquerading, knowingly or unknowingly, to the best of my knowledge and belief, as the——" He stopped and frowned. "Now, what the dickens was the name of that bird?" he said. "Pheasant, partridge, ostrich, bat, flying fish, sparrow—it's something to do with eggs. What are the eggs you eat?"

"I seldom eat eggs," said the girl quietly, "but when I do they are the eggs of the common domestic fowl."

"It ain't him," said Bones, shaking his head. "No, it's—I've got it— Plover—the Plover Light Car Company."

The girl made a note on her pad.

"I want you to get the best men in London to search out this Company. If necessary, get two private detectives, or even three. Set them to work at once, and spare no expense. I want to know who's running the company—I'd investigate the matter myself, but I'm so fearfully busy—and where their offices are. Tell the detectives," said Bones, warming to the subject, "to hang around the motor-car shops in the West End. They're bound to hear a word dropped here and there, and——"

"I quite understand," said the girl.

Bones put out his lean paw and solemnly shook the girl's hand.

"If," he said, with a tremble in his voice, "if there's a typewriter in London that knows more than you, my jolly old Marguerite, I'll eat my head."

On which lines he made his exit.

Five minutes later the girl came into the office with a slip of paper.

"The Plover Motor Car Company is registered at 604, Gracechurch Street," she said. "It has a capital of eighty thousand pounds, of which forty thousand pounds is paid up. It has works at Kenwood, in the north-west of London, and the managing director is Mr. Charles O. Soames."

Bones could only look at her open-mouthed.

"Where on earth did you discover all this surprising information, dear miss?" he asked, and the girl laughed quietly.

"I can even tell you their telephone number," she said, "because it happens to be in the Telephone Book. The rest I found in the Stock Exchange Year Book."

Bones shook his head in silent admiration.

"If there's a typewriter in London——" he began, but she had fled.

An hour later Bones had evolved his magnificent idea. It was an idea worthy of his big, generous heart and his amazing optimism.

Mr. Charles O. Soames, who sat at a littered table in his shirt-sleeves, was a man with a big shock of hair and large and heavily drooping moustache, and a black chin. He smoked a big, heavy pipe, and, at the moment Bones was announced, his busy pencil was calling into life a new company offering the most amazing prospects to the young and wealthy.

He took the card from the hands of his very plain typist, and suppressed the howl of joy which rose to his throat. For the name of Bones was known in the City of London, and it was the dream of such men as Charles O. Soames that one day they would walk from the office of Mr. Augustus Tibbetts with large parcels of his paper currency under each arm.

He jumped up from his chair and slipped on a coat, pushed the prospectus he was writing under a heap of documents—one at least of which bore a striking family likeness to a county court writ—and welcomed his visitor decorously and even profoundly.

"In *re* Plover Car," said Bones briskly. He prided himself upon coming to the point with the least possible delay.

The face of Mr. Soames fell.

"Oh, you want to buy a car?" he said. He might have truly said "the car," but under the circumstances he thought that this would be tactless.

"No, dear old company promoter," said Bones, "I do not want to buy your car. In fact, you have no cars to sell."

"We've had a lot of labour trouble," said Mr. Soames hurriedly. "You've no idea of the difficulties in production—what with the Government holding up supplies—but in a few months——"

"I know all about that," said Bones. "Now, I'm a man of affairs and a man of business."

He said this so definitely that it sounded like a threat.

"I'm putting it to you, as one City of London business person to another City of London business person, is it possible to make cars at your factory?"

Mr. Soames rose to the occasion.

"I assure you, Mr. Tibbetts," he said earnestly, "it is possible. It wants a little more capital than we've been able to raise."

This was the trouble with all Mr. Soames's companies, a long list of which appeared on a brass plate by the side of his door. None of them were sufficiently capitalised to do anything except to supply him with his fees as managing director.

Bones produced a dinky little pocket-book from his waistcoat and read his notes, or, rather, attempted to read his notes. Presently he gave it up and trusted to his memory.

"You've got forty thousand pounds subscribed to your Company," he said. "Now, I'll tell you what I'm willing to do—I will take over your shares at a price."

Mr. Soames swallowed hard. Here was one of the dreams of his life coming true.

"There are four million shares issued," Bones went on, consulting his notebook.

"Eh?" said Mr. Soames in a shocked voice.

Bones looked at his book closer.

"Is it four hundred thousand?"

"Forty thousand," said Mr. Soames gently.

"It is a matter of indifference," said Bones. "The point is, will you sell?"

The managing director of the Plover Light Car Company pursed his lips.

"Of course," he said, "the shares are at a premium—not," he added quickly, "that they are being dealt with on 'Change. We have not troubled to apply for quotations. But I assure you, my dear sir, the shares are at a premium."

Bones said nothing.

"At a small premium," said Mr. Soames hopefully.

Bones made no reply.

"At a half a crown premium," said Mr. Soames pleadingly.

"At par," said Bones, in his firmest and most business-like tones.

The matter was not settled there and then, because matters are not settled with such haste in the City of London. Bones went home to his office with a new set of notes, and wired to Hamilton, asking him to come on the following day.

It was a great scheme that Bones worked out that night, with the aid of the sceptical Miss Whitland. His desk was piled high with technical publications dealing with the motor-car industry. The fact that he was buying the Company in order to rescue a friend's investment passed entirely from his mind in the splendid dream he conjured from his dubious calculations.

The Plover car should cover the face of the earth. He read an article on mass production, showing how a celebrated American produced a thousand or a hundred thousand cars a day—he wasn't certain which—and how the car, in various parts, passed along an endless table, between lines of expectant workmen, each of whom fixed a nut or unfixed a nut, so that, when the machine finally reached its journey's end, it left the table under its own power.

Bones designed a circular table, so that, if any of the workmen forgot to fix a bar or a nut or a wheel, the error could be rectified when the car came round again. The Plover car should be a household word. Its factories should spread over North London, and every year there should be a dinner with Bones in the chair, and a beautiful secretary on his right, and Bones should make speeches announcing the amount of the profits which were to be distributed to his thousands of hands in the shape of bonuses.

Hamilton came promptly at ten o'clock, and he came violently. He flew into the office and banged a paper down on Bones's desk with the enthusiasm of one who had become the sudden possessor of money which he had not earned.

"Dear old thing, dear old thing," said Bones testily, "remember dear old Dicky Orum—preserve the decencies, dear old Ham. You're not in the Wild West now, my cheery boy."

"Bones," shouted Hamilton, "you're my mascot! Do you know what has happened?"

"Lower your voice, lower your voice, dear old friend," protested Bones. "My typewriter mustn't think I am quarrelling."

"He came last night," said Hamilton, "just as I was going to bed, and knocked me up." He was almost incoherent in his joy. "He offered me three thousand five hundred pounds for my shares, and I took it like a shot."

Bones gaped at him.

"Offered you three thousand five hundred?" he gasped. "Good heavens! You don't mean to say——"

Consider the tragedy of that moment. Here was Bones, full of great schemes for establishing a car upon the world's markets, who had in his head planned extensive works, who saw in his mind's eye vistas of long, white-covered festive boards, and heard the roar of cheering which greeted him when he rose to propose continued prosperity to the firm. Consider also that his cheque was on the table before him, already made out and signed. He was at that moment awaiting the arrival of Mr. Soames.

And then to this picture, tangible or fanciful, add Mr. Charles O. Soames himself, ushered through the door of the outer office and standing as though stricken to stone at the sight of Bones and Hamilton in consultation.

"Good morning," said Bones.

Mr. Soames uttered a strangled cry and strode to the centre of the room, his face working.

"So it was a ramp, was it?" he said. "A swindle, eh? You put this up to get your pal out of the cart?"

"My dear old——" began Bones in a shocked voice.

"I see how it was done. Well, you've had me for three thousand five hundred, and your pal's lucky. That's all I've got to say. It is the first time I've ever been caught; and to be caught by a mug like you——"

"Dear old thing, moderate your language," murmured Bones.

Mr. Soames breathed heavily through his nose, thrust his hat on the back of his head, and, without another word, strode from the office, and they heard the door slam behind him. Bones and Hamilton exchanged glances; then Bones picked up the cheque from the desk and slowly tore it up. He seemed to spend his life tearing up expensive cheques.

"What is it, Bones? What the dickens did you do?" asked the puzzled Hamilton.

"Dear old Ham," said Bones solemnly, "it was a little scheme—just a little scheme. Sit down, dear old officer," he said, after a solemn pause. "And let this be a warning to you. Don't put your money in industries, dear old Captain Hamilton. What with the state of the labour market, and the deuced ingratitude of the working classes, it's positively heartbreaking—it is, indeed, dear old Ham."

And then and there he changed the whole plan and went out of industrials for good.

Chapter 5

A Cinema Picture

Mr. Augustus Tibbetts, called "Bones," made money by sheer luck—he made more by sheer artistic judgment. That is a fact which an old friend sensed a very short time after he had renewed his acquaintance with his sometime subordinate.

Yet Bones had the curious habit of making money in quite a different way from that which he planned—as, for example, in the matter of the great oil amalgamation. In these days of aeroplane travel, when it is next to impossible to watch the comings and goings of important individuals, or even to get wind of directors' meetings, the City is apt to be a little jumpy, and to respond to wild rumours in a fashion extremely trying to the nerves of conservative brokers.

There were rumours of a fusion of interests between the Franco-Persian Oil Company and the Petroleum Consolidated—rumours which set the shares of both concerns jumping up and down like two badly trained jazzers. The directorate of both companies expressed their surprise that a credulous public could accept such stories, and both M. Jorris, the emperor of the Franco-Persian block, and George Y. Walters, the prince regent of the "Petco," denied indignantly that any amalgamation was even dreamt of.

Before these denials came along Bones had plunged into the oil market, making one of the few flutters which stand as interrogation marks against his wisdom and foresight.

He did not lose; rather, he was the winner by his adventure. The extent of his immediate gains he inscribed in his private ledger; his ultimate and bigger balance he entered under a head which had nothing to do with the oil gamble—which was just like Bones, as Hamilton subsequently remarked.

Hamilton was staying with Sanders—late Commissioner of a certain group of Territories—and Bones was the subject of conversation one morning at breakfast.

The third at the table was an exceedingly pretty girl, whom the maid called "Madame," and who opened several letters addressed to "Mrs. Sanders," but who in days not long past had been known as Patricia Hamilton.

s wonderful," said Sanders, "truly wonderful! A man I ⹀ City tells me that most of the things he touches turn ⹀ And it isn't luck or chance. Bones is developing a queer business sense."

Hamilton nodded.

"It is his romantic soul which gets him there," he said. "Bones will not look at a proposition which hasn't something fantastical behind it. He doesn't know much about business, but he's a regular whale on adventure. I've been studying him for the past month, and I'm beginning to sense his method. If he sees a logical and happy end to the romantic side of any new business, he takes it on. He simply carries the business through on the back of a dream."

The girl looked up from the coffee-pot she was handling.

"Have you made up your mind, dear?"

"About going in with Bones?" Hamilton smiled. "No, not yet. Bones is frantically insistent, has had a beautiful new Sheraton desk placed in his office, and says that I'm the influence he wants, but——"

He shook his head.

"I think I understand," said Sanders. "You feel that he is doing it all out of sheer generosity and kindness. That would be like Bones. But isn't there a chance that what he says is true—that he does want a corrective influence?"

"Maybe that is so," said Captain Hamilton doubtfully. "And then there's the money. I don't mind investing my little lot, but it would worry me to see Bones pretending that all the losses of the firm came out of his share, and a big slice of the profits going into mine."

"I shouldn't let that worry you," said his sister quietly. "Bones is too nice-minded to do anything so crude. Of course, your money is nothing compared with Bones's fortune, but why don't you join him on the understanding that the capital of the Company should be—— How much would you put in?

"Four thousand."

"Well, make the capital eight thousand. Bones could always lend the Company money. Debentures—isn't that the word?"

Sanders smiled in her face.

"You're a remarkable lady," he said. "From where on earth did you get your ideas on finance?"

She went red.

"I lunched with Bones yesterday," she said. "And here is the post."

"Silence, babbler," said Hamilton. "Before we go any farther, w̲ about this matter of partnership you were discussing with Patricia?"

The maid distributed the letters. One was addressed:

"Captin Captian Hamilton, D.S.O."

"From Bones," said Hamilton unnecessarily, and Bones's letter claimed first attention. It was a frantic and an ecstatic epistle, heavily underlined and exclaimed.

"Dear old old Ham," it ran, "you simply must join me in *magnifficant* new sceme sheme plan! Wonderfull prophits profets! The most extraordiny *chance* for a fortune. . ."

"For Heaven's sake, what's this?" asked Hamilton, handing the letter across to his sister and indicating an illegible line. "It looks like 'a bad girl's leg' to me."

"My dear!" said the shocked Mrs. Sanders, and studied the vile caligraphy. "It certainly does look like that," she admitted, "and——I see! 'Legacy' is the word."

"A bad girl's legacy is the titel of the play story picture" (Bones never crossed anything out). "There's a studyo at Tunbridge and two cameras and a fellow awfully nice fellow who understands it. A pot of money the story can be improve improved imensely. Come in it dear old man—*magnifficant* chance. See me at office eariliest earilest ealiest possible time.

> Thine in art for art sake,
> BONES

"From which I gather that Bones is taking a header into the cinema business," said Sanders. "What do you say, Hamilton?"

Hamilton thought a while.

"I'll see Bones," he said.

He arrived in Town soon after ten, but Bones had been at his office two hours earlier, for the fever of the new enterprise was upon him, and his desk was piled high with notes, memoranda, price lists and trade publications. (Bones, in his fine rage of construction, flew to the technical journals as young authors fly to the Thesaurus.)

As Hamilton entered the office, Bones glared up.

"A chair," said the young man peremptorily. "No time to be lost, dear old artist. Time is on the wing, the light is fadin', an' if we want to put this jolly old country—God bless it!—in the forefront——"

EDGAR WALLACE

Bones put down his pen and leant back in his chair.

"Ham," he said, "I had a bit of a pow-wow with your sacred and sainted sister, bless her jolly old heart. That's where the idea arose. Are you on?"

"I'm on," said Hamilton, and there was a moving scene. Bones shook his hands and spoke broken English.

"There's your perfectly twee little desk, dear old officer," he said, pointing to a massive piece of furniture facing his own. "And there's only one matter to be settled."

He was obviously uncomfortable, and Hamilton would have reached for his cheque-book, only he knew his Bones much better than to suppose that such a sordid matter as finance could cause his agitation.

"Ham," said Bones, clearing his throat and speaking with an effort, "old comrade of a hundred gallant encounters, and dear old friend——"

"What's the game?" asked Hamilton suspiciously.

"There's no game," said the depressed Bones. "This is a very serious piece of business, my jolly old comrade. As my highly respected partner, you're entitled to use the office as you like—come in when you like, go home when you like. If you have a pain in the tum-tum, dear old friend, just go to bed and trust old Bones to carry on. Use any paper that's going, help yourself to nibs—you'll find there's some beautiful nibs in that cupboard—in fact, do as you jolly well like; but——"

"But?" repeated Hamilton.

"On one point alone, dear old thing," said Bones miserably, yet heroically, "we do not share."

"What's that?" asked Hamilton, not without curiosity.

"My typewriter is my typewriter," said Bones firmly, and Hamilton laughed.

"You silly ass!" he said. "I'm not going to play with your typewriter."

"That's just what I mean," said Bones. "You couldn't have put it better, dear old friend. Thank you."

He strode across the room, gripped Hamilton's hand and wrung it.

"Dear old thing, she's too young," he said brokenly. "Hard life. . . terrible experience. . . Play with her young affections, dear old thing? No. . ."

"Who the dickens are you talking about? You said typewriter."

"I said typewriter," agreed Bones gravely. "I am speaking about my——"

A light dawned upon Hamilton.

"You mean your secretary?"

"I mean my secretary," said Bones.

"Good Heavens, Bones!" scoffed Hamilton. "Of course I shan't bother her. She's your private secretary, and naturally I wouldn't think of giving her work."

"Or orders," said Bones gently. "That's a point, dear old thing. I simply couldn't sit here and listen to you giving her orders. I should scream. I'm perfectly certain I can trust you, Ham. I know what you are with the girls, but there are times——"

"You know what I am with the girls?" said the wrathful Hamilton. "What the dickens do you know about me, you libellous young devil?"

Bones raised his hand.

"We will not refer to the past," he said meaningly and was so impressive that Hamilton began to search his mind for some forgotten peccadillo.

"All that being arranged to our mutual satisfaction, dear old partner," said Bones brightly, "permit me to introduce you."

He walked to the glass-panelled door leading to the outer office, and knocked discreetly, Hamilton watching him in wonder. He saw him disappear, closing the door after him. Presently he came out again, following the girl.

"Dear young miss," said Bones in his squeakiest voice, a sure sign of his perturbation, "permit me to introduce partner, ancient commander, gallant and painstaking, jolly old Captain Hamilton, D.S.O.—which stands, young typewriter, for Deuced Satisfactory Officer."

The girl, smiling, shook hands, and Hamilton for the first time looked her in the face. He had been amazed before by her classic beauty, but now he saw a greater intelligence than he had expected to find in so pretty a face, and, most pleasing of all, a sense of humour.

"Bones and I are very old friends," he explained.

"Hem!" said Bones severely.

"Bones?" said the girl, puzzled.

"Naturally!" murmured Bones. "Dear old Ham, be decent. You can't expect an innocent young typewriter to think of her employer as 'Bones.'"

"I'm awfully sorry," Hamilton hastened to apologise, "but you see, Bones and I——"

"Dicky Orum," murmured Bones. "Remember yourself, Ham, old indiscreet one—Mr. Tibbetts. And here's the naughty old picture-taker," he said in another tone, and rushed to offer an effusive welcome to a smart young man with long, black, wavy hair and a face reminiscent, to all students who have studied his many pictures, of Louis XV. Strangely enough, his name was Louis. He was even called Lew.

"Sit down, my dear Mr. Becksteine," said Bones. "Let me introduce you to my partner. Captain Hamilton, D.S.O.—a jolly old comrade-in-arms and all that sort of thing. My lady typewriter you know, and anyway, there's no necessity for your knowing her—— I mean," he said hastily, "she doesn't want to know you, dear old thing. Now, don't be peevish. Ham, you sit there. Becksteine will sit there. You, young miss, will sit near me, ready to take down my notes as they fall from my ingenious old brain."

In the bustle and confusion the embarrassing moment of Hamilton's introduction was forgotten. Bones had a manuscript locked away in the bottom drawer of his desk, and when he had found the key for this, and had placed the document upon the table, and when he had found certain other papers, and when the girl was seated in a much more comfortable chair—Bones fussed about like an old hen—the proceedings began.

Bones explained.

He had seen the derelict cinema company advertised in a technical journal, had been impressed with the amount of the impedimenta which accompanied the proprietorship of the syndicate, had been seized with a brilliant idea, bought the property, lock, stock, and barrel, for two thousand pounds, for which sum, as an act of grace, the late proprietors allowed him to take over the contract of Mr. Lew Becksteine, that amiable and gifted producer.

It may be remarked, in passing, that this arrangement was immensely satisfactory to the syndicate, which was so tied and bound to Mr. Becksteine for the next twelve months that to have cancelled his contract would have cost them the greater part of the purchase price which Bones paid.

"This is the story," said Bones impressively. "And, partner Ham, believe me, I've read many, many stories in my life, but never, never has one touched me as this has. It's a jolly old tear-bringer, Ham. Even a hardened, wicked old dev—old bird like you would positively dissolve. You would really, dear old Ham, so don't deny it. You know you've got one of the tenderest hearts in the world, you rascal!"

He got up and shook hands with Hamilton, though there was no necessity for him to move.

"Now, clever old Becksteine thinks that this is going to be a scorcher."

"A winner, a winner," murmured Mr. Becksteine, closing his eyes and shaking his head. He spoke on this occasion very softly, but he could raise his voice to thrilling heights. "A sure winner, my dear sir. I have been in the profession for twenty-seven years, and never in my life have I read a drama which contains so much heart appeal——"

"You hear?" said Bones in a hoarse whisper.

"—so much genuine comedy——"

Bones nodded.

"—so much that I might say goes straight to the passionate heart of the great public, as this remarkable, brilliantly planned, admirably planted, exquisitely balanced little cameo of real life."

"It's to be a two-roller," said Bones.

"Reeler," murmured Mr. Becksteine.

"Reeler or roller, dear old thing; don't let's quarrel over how a thing's spelt," said Bones.

"Who wrote it?" asked Hamilton.

Mr. Becksteine coughed modestly.

"Jolly old Becksteine wrote it," said Bones. "That man, Ham, is one of the most brilliant geniuses in this or any other world. Aren't you? Speak up, old playwright. Don't be shy, old thing."

Mr. Becksteine coughed again.

"I do not know anything about other worlds," he admitted.

"Now, this is my idea," said Bones, interrupting what promised to be a free and frank admission of Mr. Becksteine's genius. "I've worked the thing out, and I see just how we can save money. In producing two-roller cinematographs—that's the technical term," explained Bones, "the heavy expense is with the artistes. The salaries that these people are paid! My dear old Ham, you'd never believe."

"I don't see how you can avoid paying salaries," said Hamilton patiently. "I suppose even actors have to live."

"Ah!" said Mr. Becksteine, shaking his head.

"Of course, dear old thing. But why pay outside actors?" said Bones triumphantly.

He glared from one face to the other with a ferocity of expression which did no more than indicate the strength of his conviction.

"Why not keep the money in the family, dear old Ham? That's what I ask you. Answer me that." He leaned back in his chair, thrust his hands in his trousers pockets, and blandly surveyed his discomfited audience.

"But you've got to have actors, my dear chap," said Hamilton.

"Naturally and necessarily," replied Bones, nodding with very large nods. "And we have them. Who is Jasper Brown, the villain who tries to rob the poor girl of her legacy and casts the vilest aspersions upon her jolly old name?"

"Who is?" asked the innocent Hamilton.

"You are," said Bones.

Hamilton gasped.

"Who is Frank Fearnot, the young and handsome soldier—well, not necessarily handsome, but pretty good-looking—who rescues the girl from her sad predicament?"

"Well, that can't be me, anyway," said Hamilton.

"It is not," said Bones. "It is me! Who is the gorgeous but sad old innocent one who's chased by you, Ham, till the poor little soul doesn't know which way to turn, until this jolly young officer steps brightly on the scene, whistling a merry tune, and, throwing his arms about her, saves her, dear old thing, from her fate—or, really, from a perfectly awful rotten time."

"Who is she?" asked Hamilton softly.

Bones blinked and turned to the girl slowly.

"My dear old miss," he said, "what do you think?"

"What do I think?" asked the startled girl. "What do I think about what?"

"There's a part," said Bones—"there's one of the grandest parts that was ever written since Shakespeare shut his little copybook."

"You're not suggesting that I should play it?" she asked, open-mouthed.

"Made for you, dear old typewriter, positively made for you, that part," murmured Bones.

"Of course I shall do nothing so silly," said the girl, with a laugh. "Oh, Mr. Tibbetts, you really didn't think that I'd do such a——"

She didn't finish the sentence, but Hamilton could have supplied the three missing words without any difficulty.

Thereafter followed a discussion, which in the main consisted of joint and several rejection of parts. Marguerite Whitland most resolutely refused to play the part of the bad girl, even though Bones promised to change the title to "The Good Girl," even though he wheedled his best, even though he struck attitudes indicative of despair and utter ruin, even though the gentle persuasiveness of Mr. Lew Becksteine was added to his entreaties. And Hamilton as resolutely declined to have anything to do with the bad man. Mr. Becksteine solved the difficulty by undertaking to produce the necessary actors and actresses at the minimum of cost.

"Of course you won't play, Bones?" said Hamilton.

"I don't know," said Bones. "I'm not so sure, dear old thing. I've got a lot of acting talent in me, and I feel the part—that's a technical term you won't understand."

"But surely, Mr. Tibbetts," said the girl reproachfully, "you won't allow yourself to be photographed embracing a perfectly strange lady?"

Bones shrugged his shoulders.

"Art, my dear old typewriter," he said. "She'll be no more to me than a bit of wood, dear old miss. I shall embrace her and forget all about it the second after. You need have no cause for apprehension, really and truly."

"I am not at all apprehensive," said the girl coldly, and Bones followed her to her office, showering explanations of his meaning over her shoulder.

On the third day Hamilton went back to Twickenham a very weary man.

"Bones is really indefatigable," he said irritably, but yet admiringly. "He has had those unfortunate actors rehearsing in the open fields, on the highways and byways. Really, old Bones has no sense of decency. He's got one big scene which he insists upon taking in a private park. I shudder to think what will happen if the owner comes along and catches Bones and his wretched company."

Sanders laughed quietly.

"What do you think he'll do with the film?" he asked.

"Oh, he'll sell it," said Hamilton. "I tell you, Bones is amazing. He has found a City man who is interested in the film industry, a stockbroker or something, who has promised to see every bit of film as it is produced and give him advice on the subject; and, incredible as it may sound, the first half-dozen scenes that Bones has taken have passed muster."

"Who turns the handle of the camera?" asked the girl.

"Bones," said Hamilton, trying not to laugh. "He practised the revolutions on a knife-cleaning machine!"

The fourth day it rained, but the fifth day Bones took his company in a hired motor into the country, and, blissfully ignoring such admonitions as "Trespassers will be shot," he led the way over a wall to the sacred soil of an Englishman's stately home. Bones wanted the wood, because one of his scenes was laid on the edge of a wood. It was the scene where the bad girl, despairing of convincing anybody as to her inherent goodness, was taking a final farewell of the world before "leaving a life which had held nothing but sadness and misunderstanding," to quote the title which was to introduce this touching episode.

Bones found the right location, fitted up his camera, placed the yellow-faced girl—the cinema artiste has a somewhat bilious appearance when facing the lens—and began his instructions.

"Now, you walk on here, dear old Miss What's-Your-Name. You come from that tree with halting footsteps—like this, dear old thing. Watch and learn."

Bones staggered across the greensward, clasping his brow, sank on his knees, folded his arms across his chest, and looked sorrowfully at the heavens, shaking his head.

Hamilton screamed with laughter.

"Behave yourself, naughty old sceptic," said Bones severely.

After half an hour's preliminary rehearsal, the picture was taken, and Bones now prepared to depart; but Mr. Lew Becksteine, from whose hands Bones had taken, not only the direction of the play, but the very excuse for existence, let fall a few uncomfortable words.

"Excuse me, Mr. Tibbetts," he said, in the sad, bored voice of an artiste who is forced to witness the inferior work of another, "it is in this scene that the two lawyers must be taken, walking through the wood, quite unconscious of the unhappy fate which has overtaken the heiress for whom they are searching."

"True," said Bones, and scratched his nose.

He looked round for likely lawyers. Hamilton stole gently away.

"Now, why the dickens didn't you remind me, you careless old producer, to bring two lawyers with me?" asked Bones. "Dash it all, there's nothing here that looks like a lawyer. Couldn't it be taken somewhere else?"

Mr. Becksteine had reached the stage where he was not prepared to make things easy for his employer.

"Utterly impossible," he said; "you must have exactly the same scenery. The camera cannot lie."

Bones surveyed his little company, but without receiving any encouragement.

"Perhaps I might find a couple of fellows on the road," he suggested.

"It is hardly likely," said Mr. Lew Becksteine, "that you will discover in this remote country village two gentlemen arrayed in faultlessly fitting morning-coats and top-hats!"

"I don't know so much about that," said the optimistic Bones, and took a short cut through the wood, knowing that the grounds made an abrupt turn where they skirted the main road.

He was half-way through the copse when he stopped. Now, Bones was a great believer in miracles, but they had to be very spectacular miracles. The fact that standing in the middle of the woodland path were two middle-aged gentlemen in top-hats and morning-coats, seemed to Bones to be a mere slice of luck. It was, in fact, a miracle of the first class. He crept silently back, raced down the steps to where the little party stood.

"Camera!" he hissed. "Bring it along, dear old thing. Don't make a noise! Ham, old boy, will you help? You other persons, stay where you are."

Hamilton shouldered the camera, and on the way up the slope Bones revealed his fell intention.

"There is no need to tell these silly old jossers what we're doing," he said. "You see what I mean, Ham, old boy? We'll just take a picture of them as they come along. Nobody will be any the wiser, and all we'll have to do will be to put a little note in." All the time he was fixing the camera on the tripod, focussing the lens on a tree by the path. (It was amazing how quickly Bones mastered the technique of any new hobby he took up.)

From where Hamilton crouched in the bushes he could see the two men plainly. His heart quaked, realising that one at least was possibly the owner of the property on which he was trespassing; and he had all an Englishman's horror of trespass. They were talking together, these respectable gentlemen, when Bones began to turn the handle. They had to pass through a patch of sunlight, and it was upon this that Bones concentrated. Once one of them looked around as the sound of clicking came to him, but at that moment Bones decided he had taken enough and stopped.

"This," said he, as they gained the by-road where they had made their unauthorised entry into the park, "is a good day's work."

Their car was on the main road, and to Hamilton's surprise he found the two staid gentlemen regarding it when the party came up. They were regarding it from a high bank behind the wall—a bank which commanded a view of the road. One of them observed the camera and said something in a low tone to the other; then the speaker walked down the bank, opened a little wicker door in the wall, and came out.

He was a most polite man, and tactful.

"Have you been taking pictures?" he asked.

"Dear old fellow," said Bones. "I will not deceive you—we have."

There was a silence.

"In the—park, by any chance?" asked the gentleman carelessly.

Bones flinched. He felt rather guilty, if the truth be told.

"The fact is——" he began.

The elderly man listened to the story of "The Bad Girl's Legacy," its genesis, its remarkable literary qualities, and its photographic value. He seemed to know a great deal about cinematographs, and asked several questions.

"So you have an expert who sees the pieces as they are produced?" he asked. "Who is that?"

"Mr. Tim Lewis," said Bones. "He's one of the——"

"Lewis?" said the other quickly. "Is that Lewis the stockbroker? And does he see every piece you take?"

Bones was getting weary of answering questions.

"Respected sir and park proprietor," he said, "if we have trespassed, I apologise. If we did any harm innocently, and without knowing that we transgressed the jolly old conventions—if we, as I say, took a picture of you and your fellow park proprietor without a thank-you-very-much, I am sorry."

"You took me and my friend?" asked the elderly man quickly.

"I am telling you, respected sir and cross-examiner, that I took you being in a deuce of a hole for a lawyer."

"I see," said the elderly man. "Will you do me a favour? Will you let me see your copy of that picture before you show it to Mr. Lewis? As the respected park proprietor"—he smiled—"you owe me that."

"Certainly, my dear old friend and fellow-sufferer," said Bones. "Bless my life and heart and soul, certainly!"

He gave the address of the little Wardour Street studio where the film would be developed and printed, and fixed the morrow for an exhibition.

"I should very much like to see it to-night, if it is no trouble to you."

"We will certainly do our best, sir," Hamilton felt it was necessary to interfere at this point.

"Of course, any extra expense you are put to as the result of facilitating the printing, or whatever you do to these films," said the elderly man, "I shall be glad to pay."

He was waiting for Bones and Hamilton at nine o'clock that night in the dingy little private theatre which Bones, with great difficulty, had secured for his use. The printing of the picture had been accelerated, and though the print was slightly speckled, it was a good one.

The elderly man sat in a chair and watched it reeled off, and when the lights in the little theatre went up, he turned to Bones with a smile.

"I'm interested in cinema companies," he said, "and I rather fancy that I should like to include your property in an amalgamation I am making. I could assist you to fix a price," he said to the astonished Bones, "if you would tell me frankly, as I think you will, just what this business has cost you from first to last."

"My dear old amalgamator," said Bones reproachfully, "is that business? I ask you."

"It may be good business," said the other.

Bones looked at Hamilton. They and the elderly man, who had driven up to the door of the Wardour Street studio in a magnificent car, were the only three people, besides the operator, who were present.

Hamilton nodded.

"Well," said Bones, "business, dear old thing, is my weakness. Buying and selling is my passion and Lobby. From first to last, after paying jolly old Brickdust, this thing is going to cost me more than three thousand pounds—say, three thousand five hundred."

The elderly man nodded.

"Let's make a quick deal," he said. "I'll give you six thousand pounds for the whole concern, with the pictures as you have taken them—negatives, positives, cameras, etc. Is it a bargain?"

Bones held out his hand.

They dined together, a jubilant Bones and a more jubilant Hamilton, at a little restaurant in Soho.

"My dear old Ham," said Bones, "it only shows you how things happen. This would have been a grand week for me if those beastly oil shares of mine had gone up. I'm holding 'em for a rise." He opened a newspaper he had bought in the restaurant. "I see that Jorris and Walters—they're the two oil men—deny that they've ever met or that they're going to amalgamate. But can you believe these people?" he asked. "My dear old thing, the mendacity of these wretched financiers——"

"Have you ever seen them?" asked Hamilton, to whom the names of Jorris and Walters were as well known as to any other man who read his daily newspaper.

"Seen them?" said Bones. "My dear old fellow, I've met them time and time again. Two of the jolliest old birds in the world. Well, here's luck!"

At that particular moment Mr. Walters and Mr. Jorris were sitting together in the library of a house in Berkeley Square, the blinds being lowered and the curtains being drawn, and Mr. Walters was saying:

"We'll have to make this thing public on Wednesday. My dear fellow, I nearly fainted when I heard that that impossible young person had photographed us together. When do you go back to Paris?"

"I think I had better stay here," said Mr. Jorris. "Did the young man bleed you?"

"Only for six thousand," said the pleasant Mr. Walters. "I hope the young beggar's a bear in oil," he added viciously.

But Bones, as we know, was a bull.

Chapter 6

A Deal in Jute

It is a reasonable theory that every man of genius is two men, one visible, one unseen and often unsuspected by his counterpart. For who has not felt the shadow's influence in dealing with such as have the Spark? Napoleon spoke of stars, being Corsican and a mystic. Those who met him in his last days were uneasily conscious that the second Bonaparte had died on the eve of Waterloo, leaving derelict his brother, a stout and commonplace man who was in turn sycophantic, choleric, and pathetic, but never great.

Noticeable is the influence of the Shadow in the process of money-making. It is humanly impossible for some men to be fortunate. They may amass wealth by sheer hard work and hard reasoning, but if they seek a shorter cut to opulence, be sure that short cut ends in a cul-de-sac where sits a Bankruptcy Judge and a phalanx of stony-faced creditors. "Luck" is not for them—they were born single.

For others, the whole management of life is taken from their hands by their busy Second, who ranges the world to discover opportunities for his partner.

So it comes about that there are certain men, and Augustus Tibbetts—or, as he was named, "Bones"—was one of these, to whom the increments of life come miraculously. They could come in no other way, be he ever so learned and experienced.

Rather would a greater worldliness have hampered his familiar and in time destroyed its power, just as education destroys the more subtle instincts. Whilst the learned seismographer eats his dinner, cheerfully unconscious of the coming earthquake, his dog shivers beneath the table.

By this preamble I am not suggesting that Bones was a fool. Far from it. Bones was wise—uncannily wise in some respects. His success was due, as to nine-tenths, to his native sense. His x supplied the other fraction.

No better illustration of the working of this concealed quantity can be given than the story of the great jute sale and Miss Bertha Stegg.

The truth about the Government speculation in jute is simply told. It is the story of an official who, in the middle of the War, was seized with the bright idea of procuring enormous quantities of jute for the manufacture of sand-bags. The fact that by this transaction he might have driven the jute lords of Dundee into frenzy did not enter into his calculations. Nor did it occur to him that the advantageous position in which he hoped to place his Department depended for its attainment upon a total lack of foresight on the part of the Dundee merchants.

As a matter of fact, Dundee had bought well and wisely. It had sufficient stocks to meet all the demands which the Government made upon it; and when, after the War, the Department offered its purchase at a price which would show a handsome profit to the Government, Dundee laughed long and loudly.

And so there was left on the official hands, at the close of the War, a quantity of jute which nobody wanted, at a price which nobody would pay. And then somebody asked a question in the House of Commons, and the responsible Secretary went hot all over, and framed the reply which an Under-secretary subsequently made in such terms as would lead the country to believe that the jute purchased at a figure beyond the market value was a valuable asset, and would one day be sold at a profit.

Mr. Augustus Tibbetts knew nothing about jute. But he did read, almost every morning in the daily newspapers, how one person or another had made enormous purchases of linen, or of cloth, or of motor chassis, paying fabulous sums on the nail and walking off almost immediately with colossal profits; and every time Bones read such an account he wriggled in his chair and made unhappy noises.

Then one afternoon there came to his office a suave gentleman in frock-coat, carrying with him a card which was inscribed "Ministry of Supplies." And the end of that conversation was that Bones, all a twitter of excitement, drove to a gloomy office in Whitehall, where he interviewed a most sacred public official, to whom members of the public were not admitted, perhaps, more than four times a year.

Hamilton had watched the proceedings with interest and suspicion. When Bones was mysterious he was very mysterious; and he returned that night in such a condition of mystery that none but a thought-reading detective could have unravelled him.

"You seem infernally pleased with yourself, Bones," said Hamilton. "What lamentable error have you fallen into?"

"Dear old Ham," said Bones, with the helpless little laugh which characterised the very condition of mind which Hamilton had described, "dear old pryer, wait till to-morrow. Dear old thing, I wouldn't spoil it. Read your jolly old newspaper, dear old inquirer."

"Have you been to the police court?" asked Hamilton.

"Police court? Police court?" said Bones testily. "Good Heavens, lad! Why this jolly old vulgarity? No, dear boy, live and learn, dear old thing!"

Hamilton undoubtedly lived until the next morning, and learnt. He saw the headlines the second he opened his newspaper.

GREAT DEAL IN JUTE.
PROMINENT CITY MAN BUYS GOVERNMENT SUPPLY
OF JUTE FOR A MILLION.

Hamilton was on his way to the office, and fell back in the corner of the railway carriage with a suppressed moan. He almost ran to the office, to find Bones stalking up and down the room, dictating an interview to a reporter.

"One minute, one minute, dear old Ham," said Bones warningly. And then, turning to the industrious journalist, he went on where Hamilton had evidently interrupted him. "You can say that I've spent a great deal of my life in fearfully dangerous conditions," he said. "You needn't say where, dear old reporter, just say 'fearfully dangerous conditions.'"

"What about jute?" asked the young man.

"Jute," said Bones with relish, "or, as we call it, *Corcharis capsilaris*, is the famous jute tree. I have always been interested in jute and all that sort of thing—— But you know what to say better than I can tell you. You can also say that I'm young—no, don't say that. Put it like this: 'Mr. Tibbetts, though apparently young-looking, bears on his hardened old face the marks of years spent in the service of his country. There is a sort of sadness about his funny old eyes——' You know what to say, old thing."

"I know," said the journalist, rising. "You'll see this in the next edition, Mr. Tibbetts."

When the young man had gone, Hamilton staggered across to him.

"Bones," he said, in a hollow voice, "you've never bought this stuff for a million?"

"A million's a bit of an exaggeration, dear old sportsman," said Bones. "As a matter of fact, it's about half that sum, and it needn't be paid for a month. Here is the contract." He smacked his lips and smacked the contract, which was on the table, at the same time. "Don't get alarmed, don't get peevish, don't get panicky, don't be a wicked old flutterer, Ham, my boy!" he said. "I've reckoned it all out, and I shall make a cool fifty thousand by this time next week."

"What will you pay for it?" asked Hamilton, in a shaky voice. "I mean, how much a ton?"

Bones mentioned a figure, and Hamilton jotted down a note.

He had a friend, as it happened, in the jute trade—the owner of a big mill in Dundee—and to him he dispatched an urgent telegram. After that he examined the contract at leisure. On the fourth page of that interesting document was a paragraph, the seventh, to this effect:

"Either parties to this contract may, for any reason whatsoever, by giving notice either to the Ministry of Supplies, Department 9, or to the purchaser at his registered office, within twenty-four hours of the signing of this contract, cancel the same."

He read this over to Bones.

"That's rum," he said. "What is the idea?"

"My jolly old captain," said Bones in his lordly way, "how should I know? I suppose it's in case the old Government get a better offer. Anyway, dear old timidity, it's a contract that I'm not going to terminate, believe me!"

The next afternoon Bones and Hamilton returned from a frugal lunch at a near-by tavern, and reached the imposing entrance of the building in which New Schemes Limited was housed simultaneously— or perhaps it would be more truthful to say a little later—than a magnificent limousine. It was so far ahead of them that the chauffeur had time to descend from his seat, open the highly-polished door, and assist to the honoured sidewalk a beautiful lady in a large beaver coat, who carried under her arm a small portfolio.

There was a certain swing to her shoulder as she walked, a certain undulatory movement of hip, which spoke of a large satisfaction with the world as she found it.

Bones, something of a connoisseur and painfully worldly, pursed his lips and broke off the conversation in which he was engaged, and which had to do with the prospective profits on his jute deal, and remarked tersely:

"Ham, dear old thing, that is a chinchilla coat worth twelve hundred pounds."

Hamilton, to whom the mysteries of feminine attire were honest mysteries, accepted the sensational report without demur.

"The way you pick up these particular bits of information, Bones, is really marvellous to me. It isn't as though you go out a lot into society. It isn't as though women are fond of you or make a fuss of you."

Bones coughed.

"Dicky Orum. Remember, dear old Richard," he murmured. "My private life, dear old fellow, if you will forgive me snubbing you, is a matter on which nobody is an authority except A. Tibbetts, Esq. There's a lot you don't know, dear old Ham. I was thinking of writing a book about it, but it would take too long."

By this time they reached the elevator, which descended in time to receive the beautiful lady in the brown coat. Bones removed his hat, smoothed his glossy hair, and with a muttered "After you, dear old friend. Age before honesty," bundled Hamilton into the lift and followed him.

The elevator stopped at the third floor, and the lady got out. Bones, his curiosity overcoming his respect for age or his appreciation of probity, followed her, and was thrilled to discover that she made straight for his office. She hesitated for a moment before that which bore the word "Private," and passed on to the outer and general office.

Bones slipped into his own room so quickly that by the time Hamilton entered he was sitting at his desk in a thoughtful and studious attitude.

It cannot be said that the inner office was any longer entitled to the description of sanctum sanctorum. Rather was the holy of holies the larger and less ornate apartment wherein sat A Being whose capable little fingers danced over complicated banks of keys.

The communicating door opened and the Being appeared. Hamilton, mindful of a certain agreement with his partner, pretended not to see her.

"There's a lady who wishes a private interview with you, Mr. Tibbetts," said the girl.

Bones turned with an exaggerated start.

"A lady?" he said in a tone of incredulity. "Gracious Heavens! This is news to me, dear old miss. Show her in, please, show her in. A private interview, eh?" He looked meaningly at Hamilton. Hamilton did not raise his eyes—in accordance with his contract. "A private interview, eh?" said Bones louder. "Does she want to see me by myself?"

"Perhaps you would like to see her in my room," said the girl. "I could stay here with Mr. Hamilton."

Bones glared at the unconscious Hamilton.

"That is not necessary, dear old typewriter," he said stiffly. "Show the young woman in, please."

The "young woman," came in. Rather, she tripped and undulated and swayed from the outer office to the chair facing Bones, and Bones rose solemnly to greet her.

Miss Marguerite Whitland, the beautiful Being, who had surveyed the tripping and swaying and undulating with the same frank curiosity that Cleopatra might have devoted to a performing seal, went into her office and closed the door gently behind her.

"Sit down, sit down," said Bones. "And what can I do for you, young miss?"

The girl smiled. It was one of those flashing smiles which make susceptible men blink. Bones was susceptible. Never had he been gazed upon with such kindness by a pair of such large, soft, brown eyes. Never had cheeks dimpled so prettily and so pleasurably, and seldom had Bones experienced such a sensation of warm embarrassment—not unpleasant—as he did now.

"I am sure I am being an awful nuisance to you, Mr. Tibbetts," said the lady. "You don't know my name, do you? Here is my card." She had it ready in her hand, and put it in front of him. Bones waited a minute or two while he adjusted his monocle, and read:

"Miss Bertha Stegg."

As a matter of fact, he read it long before he had adjusted his monocle, but the official acknowledgment was subsequent to that performance.

"Yes, yes," said Bones, who on such occasions as these, or on such occasions as remotely resembled these, was accustomed to take on the air and style of the strong, silent man. "What can we do for you, my jolly old—Miss Stegg?"

"It's a charity," blurted the girl, and sat back to watch the effect of her words. "Oh, I know what you business men are! You simply hate people bothering you for subscriptions! And really, Mr. Tibbetts, if I had to come to ask you for money, I would never have come at all. I think it's so unfair for girls to pester busy men in their offices, at the busiest time of the day, with requests for subscriptions."

Bones coughed. In truth, he had never been pestered, and was enjoying the experience.

"No, this is something much more pleasant, from my point of view," said the girl. "We are having a bazaar in West Kensington on behalf of the Little Tots' Recreation Fund."

"A most excellent plan," said Bones firmly.

Hamilton, an interested audience, had occasion to marvel anew at the amazing self-possession of his partner.

"It is one of the best institutions that I know," Bones went on thoughtfully. "Of course, it's many years since I was a little tot, but I can still sympathise with the jolly old totters, dear young miss."

She had taken her portfolio from under her arm and laid it on his desk. It was a pretty portfolio, bound in powder blue and silver, and was fastened by a powder blue tape with silver tassels. Bones eyed it with pardonable curiosity.

"I'm not asking you for money, Mr. Tibbetts," Miss Stegg went on in her soft, sweet voice. "I think we can raise all the money we want at the bazaar. But we must have things to sell."

"I see, dear old miss," said Bones eagerly. "You want a few old clothes? I've got a couple of suits at home, rather baggy at the knees, dear old thing, but you know what we boys are; we wear 'em until they fall off!"

The horrified Hamilton returned to the scrutiny of his notes.

"I don't suppose under-garments, if you will permit the indelicacy, my dear old philanthropist——" Bones was going on, when the girl stopped him with a gentle shake of her head.

"No, Mr. Tibbetts, it is awfully kind of you, but we do not want anything like that. The way we expect to raise a lot of money is by selling the photographs of celebrities," she said.

"The photographs of celebrities?" repeated Bones. "But, my dear young miss, I haven't had my photograph taken for years."

Hamilton gasped. He might have gasped again at what followed, but for the fact that he had got a little beyond the gasping stage.

The girl was untying her portfolio, and now she produced something and laid it on the desk before Bones.

"How clever of you to guess!" she murmured. "Yes, it is a portrait of you we want to sell."

Bones stared dumbfounded at a picture of himself—evidently a snapshot taken with a press camera—leaving the building. And, moreover, it was a flattering picture, for there was a stern frown of resolution on Bones's pictured face, which, for some esoteric reason, pleased him. The picture was mounted rather in than on cardboard, for it was in a sunken mount, and beneath the portrait was a little oblong slip of pale blue paper.

Bones gazed and glowed. Neatly printed above the picture were the words: "Our Captains of Industry. III.—Augustus Tibbetts, Esq. (Schemes Limited)."

Bones read this with immense satisfaction. He wondered who were the two men who could be placed before him, but in his generous mood was prepared to admit that he might come third in the list of London's merchant princes.

"Deuced flattering, dear old thing," he murmured. "Hamilton, old boy, come and look at this."

Hamilton crossed to the desk, saw, and wondered.

"Not so bad," said Bones, dropping his head to one side and regarding the picture critically. "Not at all bad, dear old thing. You've seen me in that mood, I think, old Ham."

"What is the mood?" said Hamilton innocently. "Indigestion?"

The girl laughed.

"Let's have a little light on the subject," said Bones. "Switch on the expensive old electricity, Ham."

"Oh, no," said the girl quickly. "I don't think so. If you saw the picture under the light, you'd probably think it wasn't good enough, and then I should have made my journey in vain. Spare me that, Mr. Tibbetts!"

Mr. Tibbetts giggled. At that moment the Being re-appeared. Marguerite Whitland, chief and only stenographer to the firm of Schemes Limited, and Bones beckoned her.

"Just cast your eye over this, young miss," he said. "What do you think of it?"

The girl came round the group, looked at the picture, and nodded.

"Very nice," she said, and then she looked at the girl.

"Selling it for a charity," said Bones carelessly. "Some silly old josser will put it up in his drawing-room, I suppose. You know, Ham, dear old thing, I never can understand this hero-worship business. And now, my young and philanthropic collector, what do you want me to do? Give you permission? It is given."

"I want you to give me your autograph. Sign down there,"—she pointed to a little space beneath the picture—"and just let me sell it for what I can get."

"With all the pleasure in life," said Bones.

He picked up his long plumed pen and splashed his characteristic signature in the space indicated.

And then Miss Marguerite Whitland did a serious thing, an amazingly audacious thing, a thing which filled Bones's heart with horror and dismay.

Before Bones could lift the blotting pad, her forefinger had dropped upon the signature and had been drawn across, leaving nothing more than an indecipherable smudge.

"My dear old typewriter!" gasped Bones. "My dear old miss! Confound it all! Hang it all, I say! Dear old thing!"

"You can leave this picture, madam——"

"Miss," murmured Bones from force of habit. Even in his agitation he could not resist the temptation to interrupt.

"You can leave this picture, Miss Stegg," said the girl coolly. "Mr. Tibbetts wants to add it to his collection."

Miss Stegg said nothing.

She had risen to her feet, her eyes fixed on the girl's face, and, with no word of protest or explanation, she turned and walked swiftly from the office. Hamilton opened the door, noting the temporary suspension of the undulatory motion.

When she had gone, they looked at one another, or, rather, they looked at the girl, who, for her part, was examining the photograph. She took a little knife from the desk before Bones and inserted it into the thick cardboard mount, and ripped off one of the layers of cardboard. And so Bones's photograph was exposed, shorn of all mounting. But, what was more important, beneath his photograph was a cheque on the Third National Bank, which was a blank cheque and bearing Bones's undeniable signature in the bottom right-hand corner—the signature was decipherable through the smudge.

Bones stared.

"Most curious thing I've ever seen in my life, dear old typewriter," he said. "Why, that's the very banking establishment I patronise."

"I thought it might be," said the girl.

And then it dawned upon Bones, and he gasped.

"Great Moses!" he howled—there is no prettier word for it. "That naughty, naughty, Miss Thing-a-me-jig was making me sign a blank cheque! My autograph! My sacred aunt! Autograph on a cheque. . ."

Bones babbled on as the real villainy of the attempt upon his finances gradually unfolded before his excited vision.

Explanations were to follow. The girl had seen a paragraph warning people against giving their autographs, and the police had even circulated a rough description of two "well-dressed women" who, on one pretext or another, were securing from the wealthy, but the unwise, specimens of their signatures.

"My young and artful typewriter," said Bones, speaking with emotion, "you have probably saved me from utter ruin, dear old thing. Goodness only knows what might have happened, or where I might have been sleeping to-night, my jolly old Salvationist, if your beady little eye hadn't penetrated like a corkscrew through the back of that naughty old lady's neck and read her evil intentions."

"I don't think it was a matter of my beady eye," said the girl, without any great enthusiasm for the description, "as my memory."

"I can't understand it," said Bones, puzzled. "She came in a beautiful car——"

"Hired for two hours for twenty-five shillings," said the girl.

"But she was so beautifully dressed. She had a chinchilla coat——"

"Imitation beaver," said Miss Marguerite Whitland, who had few illusions. "You can get them for fifteen pounds at any of the West End shops."

It was a very angry Miss Bertha Stegg who made her way in some haste to Pimlico. She shared a first-floor suite with a sister, and she burst unceremoniously into her relative's presence, and the elder Miss Stegg looked round with some evidence of alarm.

"What's wrong?" she asked.

She was a tall, bony woman, with a hard, tired face, and lacked most of her sister's facial charm.

"Turned down," said Bertha briefly. "I had the thing signed, and then a——" (one omits the description she gave of Miss Marguerite Whitland, which was uncharitable) "smudged the thing with her fingers."

"She tumbled to it, eh?" said Clara. "Has she put the splits on you?"

"I shouldn't think so," said Bertha, throwing off her coat and her hat, and patting her hair. "I got away too quickly, and I came on by the car."

"Will he report it to the police?"

"He's not that kind. Doesn't it make you mad, Clara, to think that that fool has a million to spend? Do you know what he's done? Made perhaps a hundred thousand pounds in a couple of days! Wouldn't that rile you?"

They discussed Bones in terms equally unflattering. They likened Bones to all representatives of the animal world whose characteristics are extreme foolishness, but at last they came into a saner, calmer frame of mind.

Miss Clara Stegg seated herself on the frowsy sofa—indispensable to a Pimlico furnished flat—and, with her elbow on one palm and her chin on another, reviewed the situation. She was the brains of a little combination which had done so much to distress and annoy susceptible financiers in the City of London. (The record of the Stegg sisters may be read by the curious, or, at any rate, by as many of the curious as have the *entrée* to the Record Department of Scotland Yard.)

The Steggs specialised in finance, and operated exclusively in high financial circles. There was not a fluctuation of the market which Miss Clara Stegg did not note; and when Rubber soared sky-high, or Steel Preferred sagged listlessly, she knew just who was going to be affected, and just how approachable they were.

During the War the Stegg sisters had opened a new department, so to speak, dealing with Government contracts, and the things which they knew about the incomes of Government contractors the average surveyor of taxes would have given money to learn.

"It was my mistake, Bertha," she said at last, "though in a sense it wasn't. I tried him simply, because he's simple. If you work something complicated on a fellow like that, you're pretty certain to get him guessing."

She went out of the room, and presently returned with four ordinary exercise-books, one of which she opened at a place where a page was covered with fine writing, and that facing was concealed by a sheet of letter-paper which had been pasted on to it. The letter-paper bore the embossed heading of Schemes Limited, the epistle had reference to a request for an autograph which Bones had most graciously granted.

The elder woman looked at the signature, biting her nether lip.

"It is almost too late now. What is the time?" she asked.

"Half-past three," replied her sister.

Miss Stegg shook her head.

"The banks are closed, and, anyway——"

She carried the book to a table, took a sheet of paper and a pen, and, after a close study of Bones's signature, she wrote it, at first awkwardly, then, after about a dozen attempts, she produced a copy which it was difficult to tell apart from the original.

"Really, Clara, you're a wonder," said her sister admiringly.

Clara made no reply. She sat biting the end of the pen.

"I hate the idea of getting out of London and leaving him with all that money, Bertha," she said. "I wonder——" She turned to her sister. "Go out and get all the evening newspapers," she said. "There's bound to be something about him, and I might get an idea."

There was much about Bones in the papers the younger girl brought, and in one of these journals there was quite an important interview, which gave a sketch of Bones's life, his character, and his general appearance. Clara read this interview very carefully.

"It says he's spent a million, but I know that's a lie," she said. "I've been watching that jute deal for a long time, and it's nearer half the sum." She frowned. "I wonder——" she said.

"Wonder what?" asked the younger girl impatiently. "What's the good of wondering? The only thing we can do is to clear out."

Again Clara went from the room and came back with an armful of documents. These she laid on the table, and the girl, looking down, saw that they were for the main part blank contracts. Clara turned them over and over until at last she came to one headed "Ministry of Supplies."

"This'd be the form," she said. "It is the same that Stevenhowe had."

She was mentioning the name of a middle-aged man, who, quite unwittingly and most unwillingly, had contributed to her very handsome bank balance. She scanned the clauses through, and then flung down the contract in disgust.

"There's nothing mentioned about a deposit," she said, "and, anyway, I doubt very much whether I could get it back, even on his signature."

A quarter of an hour later Miss Clara Stegg took up the contract again and read the closely-printed clauses very carefully. When she had finished she said:

"I just hate the idea of that fellow making money."

"You've said that before," said her sister tartly.

At six o'clock that evening Bones went home. At nine o'clock he was sitting in his sitting-room in Clarges Street—a wonderful place, though small, of Eastern hangings and subdued lights—when Hamilton burst in upon him; and Bones hastily concealed the poem he was writing and thrust it under his blotting-pad. It was a good poem and going well.

It began:

How very sweet
Is Marguerite!

And Bones was, not unreasonably, annoyed at this interruption to his muse.

As to Hamilton, he was looking ill.

"Bones," said Hamilton quietly, "I've had a telegram from my pal in Dundee. Shall I read it?"

"Dear old thing," said Bones, with an irritated "tut-tut," "really, dear old creature, at this time of night—your friends in Dundee—really, my dear old boy——"

"Shall I read it?" said Hamilton, with sinister calm.

"By all means, by all means," said Bones, waving an airy hand and sitting back with resignation written on every line of his countenance.

"Here it is," said Hamilton. "It begins 'Urgent.'"

"That means he's in a devil of a hurry, old thing," said Bones, nodding.

"And it goes on to say," said Hamilton, ignoring the interruption. "'Your purchase at the present price of jute is disastrous. Jute will never again touch the figure at which your friend tendered, Ministry have been trying to find a mug for years to buy their jute, half of which is spoilt by bad warehousing, as I could have told you, and I reckon you have made a loss of exactly half the amount you have paid.'"

Bones had opened his eyes and was sitting up.

"Dear old Job's comforter," he said huskily.

"Wait a bit," said Hamilton, "I haven't finished yet," and went on: "'Strongly advise you cancel your sale in terms of Clause 7 Ministry contract.' That's all," said Hamilton.

"Oh, yes," said Bones feebly, as he ran his finger inside his collar, "that's all!"

"What do you think, Bones?" said Hamilton gently.

"Well, dear old cloud on the horizon," said Bones, clasping his bony knee, "it looks remarkably like serious trouble for B. Ones, Esquire. It does indeed. Of course," he said, "you're not in this, old Ham. This was a private speculation——"

"Rot!" said Hamilton contemptuously. "You're never going to try a dirty trick like that on me? Of course I'm in it. If you're in it, I'm in it."

Bones opened his mouth to protest, but subsided feebly. He looked at the clock, sighed, and lowered his eyes again.

"I suppose it's too late to cancel the contract now?"

Bones nodded.

"Twenty-four hours, poor old victim," he said miserably, "expired at five P.M."

"So that's that," said Hamilton.

Walking across, he tapped his partner on the shoulder.

"Well, Bones, it can't be helped, and probably our pal in Dundee has taken an extravagant view."

"Not he," said Bones, "not he, dear old cheerer. Well, we shall have to cut down expenses, move into a little office, and start again, dear old Hamilton."

"It won't be so bad as that."

"Not quite so bad as that," admitted Bones. "But one thing," he said with sudden energy, "one thing, dear old thing, I'll never part with. Whatever happens, dear old boy, rain or shine, sun or moon, stars or any old thing like that"—he was growing incoherent—"I will never leave my typewriter, dear old thing. I will never desert her—never, never, never, never, never!"

He turned up in the morning, looking and speaking chirpily. Hamilton, who had spent a restless night, thought he detected signs of similar restlessness in Bones.

Miss Marguerite Whitland brought him his letters, and he went over them listlessly until he came to one large envelope which bore on its flap the all-too-familiar seal of the Ministry. Bones looked at it and made a little face.

"It's from the Ministry," said the girl.

Bones nodded.

"Yes, my old notetaker," he said, "my poor young derelict, cast out"—his voice shook—"through the rapacious and naughty old speculations of one who should have protected your jolly old interests, it is from the Ministry."

"Aren't you going to open it?" she asked.

"No, dear young typewriter, I am not," Bones said firmly. "It's all about the beastly jute, telling me to take it away. Now, where the dickens am I going to put it, eh? Never talk to me about jute," he said violently. "If I saw a jute tree at this moment, I'd simply hate the sight of it!"

She looked at him in astonishment.

"Why, whatever's wrong?" she asked anxiously.

"Nothing," said Bones. "Nothing," he added brokenly. "Oh, nothing, dear young typewriting person."

She paused irresolutely, then picked up the envelope and cut open the flap.

Remember that she knew nothing, except that Bones had made a big purchase, and that she was perfectly confident—such was her sublime faith in Augustus Tibbetts—that he would make a lot of money as a result of that purchase.

Therefore the consternation on her face as she read its contents.

"Why," she stammered, "you've never done—— Whatever made you do that?"

"Do what?" said Bones hollowly. "What made me do it? Greed, dear old sister, just wicked, naughty greed."

"But I thought," she said, bewildered, "You were going to make so much out of this deal?"

"Ha, ha," said Bones without mirth.

"But weren't you?" she asked.

"I don't think so," said Bones gently.

"Oh! So that was why you cancelled the contract?"

Hamilton jumped to his feet.

"Cancelled the contract?" he said incredulously.

"Cancelled the contract?" squeaked Bones. "What a naughty old story-teller you are!"

"But you have," said the girl. "Here's a note from the Ministry, regretting that you should have changed your mind and taken advantage of Clause Seven. The contract was cancelled at four forty-nine."

Bones swallowed something.

"This is spiritualism," he said solemnly. "I'll never say a word against jolly old Brigham Young after this!"

In the meantime two ladies who had arrived in Paris, somewhat weary and bedraggled, were taking their morning coffee outside the Café de la Paix.

"Anyway, my dear," said Clara viciously, in answer to her sister's plaint, "we've given that young devil a bit of trouble. Perhaps they won't renew the contract, and anyway, it'll take a bit of proving that he did not sign that cancellation I handed in."

As a matter of fact, Bones never attempted to prove it.

Chapter 7

DETECTIVE BONES

M r. Harold de Vinne was a large man, who dwelt at the dead end of a massive cigar.

He was big and broad-shouldered, and automatically jovial. Between the hours of 6 P.M. and 2 A.M. he had earned the name of "good fellow," which reputation he did his best to destroy between 10 A.M. and 4 P.M.

He was one of four stout fellows who controlled companies of imposing stability—the kind of companies that have such items in their balance sheets as "Sundry Debtors, £107,402 12s. 7d." People feel, on reading such airy lines, that the company's assets are of such magnitude that the sundry debtors are only included as a careless afterthought.

Mr. de Vinne was so rich that he looked upon any money which wasn't his as an illegal possession; and when Mr. Augustus Tibbetts, on an occasion, stepped in and robbed him of £17,500, Mr. de Vinne's family doctor was hastily summoned (figuratively speaking; literally, he had no family, and swore by certain patent medicines), and straw was spread before the temple of his mind.

A certain Captain Hamilton, late of H.M. Houssas, but now a partner in the firm of Tibbetts & Hamilton, Ltd., after a short, sharp bout of malaria, went off to Brighton to recuperate, and to get the whizzy noises out of his head. To him arrived on a morning a special courier in the shape of one Ali, an indubitable Karo boy, but reputedly pure Arab, and a *haj*, moreover, entitled to the green scarf of the veritable pilgrimage to Mecca.

Ali was the body-servant of Augustus Tibbetts, called by his intimates "Bones," and he was arrayed in the costume which restaurateurs insist is the everyday kit of a true Easterner—especially such Easterners as serve after-dinner coffee.

Hamilton, not in the best of tempers—malaria leaves you that way— and dazzled by this apparition in scarlet and gold, blinked.

"O man," he said testily in the Arabic of the Coast, "why do you walk-in-the world dressed like a so-and-so?" (You can be very rude in Arabic especially in Coast Arabic garnished with certain Swahili phrases.)

"Sir," said Ali, "these garmentures are expressly designated by Tibbetti. Embellishments of oriferous metal give wealthiness of appearance to subject, but attract juvenile research and investigation."

Hamilton glared through the window on to the front, where a small but representative gathering of the juvenile research committee waited patiently for the reappearance of one whom in their romantic fashion they had termed "The Rajah of Bong."

Hamilton took the letter and opened it. It was, of course, from Bones, and was extremely urgent. Thus it went:

"Dear Old Part.,

Ham I've had an offer of Browns you know the big big Boot shop several boot shop all over London London. Old Browns going out going out of the bisiness Sindicate trying to buy so I niped in for 105,000 pounds got lock stock and barrill baril. Sindicate awfuly sore awfuley sore. All well here except poor young typewrighter cut her finger finger sliceing bread doctor says not dangerus."

Hamilton breathed quickly. He gathered that Bones had bought a boot-shop—even a collection of boot-shops—and he was conscious of the horrible fact that Bones knew nothing about boots.

He groaned. He was always groaning, he thought, and seldom with good reason.

Bones was in a buying mood. A week before he had bought *The Weekly Sunspot*, which was "A Satirical Weekly Review of Human Affairs." The possibilities of that purchase had made Hamilton go hot and moisty. He had gone home one evening, leaving Bones dictating a leading article which was a violent attack on the Government of the day, and had come in the following morning to discover that the paper had been resold at a thousand pounds profit to the owners of a rival journal which described itself as "A Weekly Symposium of Thought and Fancy."

But Boots. . . and £105,000. . . !

This was serious. Yet there was no occasion for groaning or doubt or apprehension; for, even whilst Hamilton was reading the letter, Bones was shaking his head violently at Mr. de Vinne, of the Phit-Phine Shoe Syndicate, who had offered him £15,000 profit on the turn-over. And at the identical moment that Hamilton was buying his ticket for London, Bones was solemnly shaking hands with the Secretary of the Phit-Phine Shoe Syndicate (Mr. de Vinne having violently, even apoplectically, refused to meet Bones) with one hand, and holding in the other a cheque which represented a profit of £17,500. It was one of Bones's big deals, and reduced Hamilton to a condition of blind confidence in his partner. . . Nevertheless. . .

A week later, Bones, reading his morning paper, reached and passed, without receiving any very violent impression, the information that Mr. John Siker, the well-known private detective, had died at his residence at Clapham Park. Bones read the item without interest. He was looking for bargains—an early morning practice of his because the buying fever was still upon him.

Hamilton, sitting at his desk, endeavouring to balance the firm's accounts from a paying-in book and a cheque-book, the counterfoils of which were only occasionally filled in, heard the staccato "Swindle! . . . Swindle!" and knew that Bones had reached the pages whereon were displayed the prospectuses of new companies.

He had the firm conviction that all new companies were founded on frauds and floated by criminals. The offer of seven per cent. debenture stock moved him to sardonic laughter. The certificates of eminent chartered accountants brought a meaning little smile to his lips, followed by the perfectly libellous statement that "These people would do anything for money, dear old thing."

Presently Bones threw down the paper.

"Nothing, absolutely nothing," he said, and walked to the door of the outer office, knocked upon it, and disappeared into the sanctum of the lady whom Bones never referred to except in terms of the deepest respect as his "young typewriter!"

"Young miss," he said, pausing deferentially at the door, "may I come in?"

She smiled up at him—a proceeding which was generally sufficient to throw Bones into a pitiful condition of incoherence. But this morning it had only the effect of making him close his eyes as though to shut out a vision too radiant to be borne.

"Aren't you well, Mr. Tibbetts?" she asked quickly and anxiously.

"It's nothing, dear old miss," said Bones, passing a weary and hypocritical hand across his brow. "Just a fit of the jolly old staggers. The fact is, I've been keeping late hours—in fact, dear young miss," he said huskily, "I have been engaged in a wicked old pursuit—yes, positively naughty. . ."

"Oh, Mr. Tibbetts"—she was truly shocked—"I'm awfully sorry! You really shouldn't drink—you're so young. . ."

"Drink!" said the hurt and astounded Bones. "Dear old slanderer! Poetry!"

He had written sufficient poetry to make a volume—poems which abounded in such rhymes as "Marguerite," "Dainty feet," "Sweet," "Hard to beat," and the like. But this she did not know.

By this time the girl was not only accustomed to these periodical embarrassments of Bones, but had acquired the knack of switching the conversation to the main line of business.

"There's a letter from Mr. de Vinne," she said.

Bones rubbed his nose and said, "Oh!"

Mr. de Vinne was on his mind rather than on his conscience, for Mr. de Vinne was very angry with Bones, who, as he had said, had "niped" in and had cost Mr. de Vinne £17,500.

"It is not a nice letter," suggested the girl.

"Let me see, dear young head-turner," said Bones firmly.

The letter called him "Sir," and went on to speak of the writer's years of experience as a merchant of the City of London, in all of which, said the writer, he had never heard of conduct approaching in infamy that of Augustus Tibbetts, Esquire.

> "It has been brought to my recollection" (wrote the infuriated Mr. de Vinne) "that on the day you made your purchase of Browns, I dined at the Kingsway Restaurant, and that you occupied a table immediately behind me. I can only suppose that you overheard a *perfectly confidential*" (heavily underscored) "conversation between myself and a fellow-director, and utilised the information thus *disgracefully* acquired."

"Never talk at meals, dear old typewriter," murmured Bones. "Awfully bad for your jolly young tum—for your indigestion, dear young keytapper."

The letter went on to express the writer's intention of taking vengeance for the "dishonest squeeze" of which he had been the victim.

Bones looked at his secretary anxiously. The censure of Mr. de Vinne affected him not at all. The possible disapproval of this lady filled him with dire apprehension.

"It's not a nice letter," said the girl. "Do you want me to answer it?"

"Do I want you to answer it?" repeated Bones, taking courage. "Of course I want you to answer it, my dear old paper-stainer and decorator. Take these words."

He paced the room with a terrible frown.

"Dear old thing," he began.

"Do you want me to say 'Dear old thing'?" asked the girl.

"No, perhaps not, perhaps not," said Bones. "Start it like this: 'My dear peevish one——"

The girl hesitated and then wrote down: "Dear Sir."

"'You are just showing your naughty temper,'" dictated Bones, and added unnecessarily, "t-e-m-p-e-r."

It was a practice of his to spell simple words.

"You are just showing your naughty temper," he went on, "and I simply refuse to have anything more to do with you. You're being simply disgusting. Need I say more?" added Bones.

The girl wrote: "Dear Sir,—No useful purpose would be served either in replying to your letter of to-day's date, or re-opening the discussion on the circumstances of which you complain."

Bones went back to his office feeling better. Hamilton left early that afternoon, so that when, just after the girl had said "Good night," and Bones himself was yawning over an evening paper, and there came a rap at the door of the outer office, he was quite alone.

"Come in!" he yelled, and a young man, dressed in deep mourning, eventually appeared through the door sacred to the use of Miss Marguerite Whitland.

"I'm afraid I've come rather late in the day."

"I'm afraid you have, dear old thing," said Bones. "Come and sit down, black one. Deepest sympathy and all that sort of thing."

The young man licked his lips. His age was about twenty-four, and he had the appearance of being a semi-invalid, as, indeed, he was.

"It's rather late to see you on this matter," he said, "but your name was only suggested to me about an hour ago."

Bones nodded. Remember that he was always prepared for a miracle, even at closing time.

"My name is Siker," said the visitor.

"And a jolly good name, too," said Bones, dimly conscious of the fact that he had heard this name mentioned before.

"You probably saw the account of my father's death. It was in this morning's newspaper, though he died last week," said Mr. Siker.

Bones screwed up his forehead.

"I remember that name," he said. "Now, let me think. Why, of course—Siker's Detective Agency."

It was the young man's turn to nod.

"That's right, sir," he said. "John Siker was my father. I'm his only son."

Bones waited.

"I've heard it said, Mr. Tibbetts," said the young man—"at least, it has been represented to me—that you are on the look-out for likely businesses that show a profit."

"That's right," agreed Bones; "that show me a big profit," he added.

"Well, Siker's Detective Agency has made two thousand a year clear for twenty years," said the young man. "We've got one of the best lists of clients in the kingdom, and almost every big business man in the City is on our list. With a little more attention than my father has been able to give to it for the last two years, there's a fortune in it."

Bones was sitting upright now, his eyes shining. The amazing possibilities of such an acquisition were visible to his romantic eye.

"You want to sell it, my poor old Sherlock?" he demanded, then, remembering the part he was called upon to play, shook his head. "No, no, old thing. Deeply sorry and all that sort of thing, but it can't be done. It's not my line of business at all—not," he added, "that I don't know a jolly sight more about detectivising than a good many of these clever ones. But it's really not my game. What did you want for it?"

"Well," said the young man, hesitating, "I thought that three years' purchase would be a bargain for the man who bought it."

"Six thousand pounds," said Bones.

"Yes," agreed the other. "Of course, I won't ask you to buy the thing blindfolded. You can put the accounts in the hands of your lawyer or your accountant, and you will find that what I have said is true—that my father took two thousand a year out of his business for years. It's possible to make it four thousand. And as to running it, there are three men who do all the work—or, rather, one, Hilton, who's in charge of the office and gives the other fellows their instructions."

"But why sell it, my sad old improvidence?" said Bones. "Why chuck away two thousand a year for six thousand cash?"

"Because I'm not well enough to carry it on," said young Mr. Siker, after a moment's hesitation. "And, besides, I can't be bothered. It interferes, with my other profession—I'm a musician."

"And a jolly good profession, too," said Bones, shaking hands with him across the table. "I'll sleep on this. Give me your address and the address of your accountants, and I'll come over and see you in the morning."

Hamilton was at his desk the next morning at ten o'clock. Bones did not arrive until eleven, and Bones was monstrously preoccupied. When Hamilton saluted him with a cheery "Good morning," Bones returned a grave and non-committal nod. Hamilton went on with his work until he became conscious that somebody was staring at him, and, looking up, caught Bones in the act.

"What the devil are you looking at?" asked Hamilton.

"At your boots," was the surprising reply.

"My boots?" Hamilton pulled them back through the kneehole of the desk and looked at them. "What's the matter with the boots?"

"Mud-stains, old carelessness," said Bones tersely. "You've come from Twickenham this morning."

"Of course I've come from Twickenham. That's where I live," said Hamilton innocently. "I thought you knew that."

"I should have known it," said Bones, with great gravity, "even if I hadn't known it, so to speak. You may have observed, my dear Hamilton, that the jolly old mud of London differs widely—that is to say, is remarkably different. For instance, the mud of Twickenham is different from the mud of Balham. There's what you might call a subtle difference, dear junior partner, which an unimaginative old rascal like you wouldn't notice. Now, the mud of Peckham," said Bones, waving his forefinger, "is distinguished by a certain darkness——"

"Wait a bit," said Hamilton. "Have you bought a mud business or something?"

"No," said Bones.

"And yet this conversation seems familiar to me," mused Hamilton. "Proceed with your argument, good gossip."

"My argument," said Bones, "is that you have Twickenham mud on your boots, therefore you come from Twickenham. It is evident that on your way to the station you stopped to buy a newspaper, that something was on your mind, something made you very thoughtful—something on your jolly old conscience, I'll bet!"

"How do you know that?" asked Hamilton.

"There's your *Times* on the table," said Bones triumphantly, "unopened."

"Quite true," said Hamilton; "I bought it just before I came into the office."

"H'm!" said Bones. "Well, I won't deceive you, dear old partner. I've bought Siker's."

Hamilton put down his pen and leaned back in his chair.

"Who's Siker's?"

"Siker's Detective Agency," began Bones, "is known from one end——"

"Oh, I see. Whew!" whistled Hamilton. "You were doing a bit of detecting!"

Bones smirked.

"Got it at once, my dear old person," he said. "You know my methods——"

Hamilton's accusing eye met his, and Bones coughed.

"But what on earth do you expect to do with a detective agency, Bones?" asked Hamilton, strolling across and lighting a cigarette. "That's a type of business there isn't any big demand for. And how is it going to affect you personally? You don't want your name associated with that sort of thing."

Bones explained. It was a property he could "sit on." Bones had always been looking for such a business. The management was capable of carrying on, and all that Bones need do was to sit tight and draw a dividend.

As to his name, he had found a cunning solution to that difficulty.

"I take it over, by arrangement with the lawyer in the name of 'Mr. Senob,' and I'll bet you won't guess, dear old Ham, how I got that name!"

"It's 'Bones' spelt backwards," said Hamilton patiently. "You tried that bit of camouflage on me years ago."

Bones sniffed disappointedly and went on.

For once he was logical, brief in his explanation, and convincing. Yet Hamilton was not altogether convinced. He was waiting for the inevitable "but," and presently it came.

"But of course I'm not going to leave it entirely alone, old Ham," said Bones, shrugging his shoulders at the absurdity of such a suggestion. "The business can be doubled if a man with a capable, up-to-date conception of modern crime——"

Hamilton made a hooting noise, derisive and insulting.

"Meaning you?" he said, at the conclusion of his lamentable exhibition.

"Meaning me, Ham, my fat old sceptic," said Bones gently. "I don't think, dear old officer, you quite realise just what I know about criminal investigation."

"You silly ass," said Hamilton, "detective agencies don't criminally investigate. That's done by the real police. Detective agencies are merely employed by suspicious wives to follow their husbands."

"Exactly," said Bones, nodding. "And that is just where I come in. You see, I did a little bit of work last night—rather a pretty little bit of work." He took a slip of paper from his pocket. "You dined at the Criterion at half-past eight with a tall, fair lady—a jolly old dear she was too, old boy, and I congratulate you most heartily—named Vera."

Hamilton's face went red.

"You left the restaurant at ten past nine, and entered cab No. 667432. Am I right, sir?"

"Do you mean to tell me," exploded Hamilton, "that you were watching me?"

Bones nodded.

"I picked you up, old thing, outside the Piccadilly Tube. I shadowed you to the theatre. I followed you home. You got a taxi—No. 297431—and you were an awful long time before you got out when you reached the lady's destination—an awful long time," said Bones emphatically. "What you could find to talk about after the cab had drawn up at the dear old ancestral home of Vera——"

"Bones," said Hamilton awfully. "I think you've gone far enough."

"I thought you'd gone a bit too far, dear old thing, I did really," said Bones, shaking his head reprovingly. "I watched you very carefully."

He danced, with a little squeak of joy, into the office of his beautiful secretary, leaving a very red and a pardonably annoyed Hamilton breathing heavily.

Bones went to the office of Siker's Detective Agency early the next morning. He went, it may be remarked in passing, though these details can only be interesting to the psychologist, wearing the darkest of his dark suits and a large black wideawake hat. There was a certain furtiveness in his movements between the taxicab and the entrance of the office, which might suggest to anybody who had taken the trouble to observe him that he was an escaping bank-robber.

Siker's had spacious offices and a small staff. Only Hilton, the manager, and a clerk were in when Bones presented his card. He was immediately conducted by Mr. Hilton to a very plain inner office, surrounded with narrow shelves, which in turn were occupied by innumerable little deed boxes.

Mr. Hilton was a sober-faced man of fifty-five, sallow and unhappy. His tone was funereal and deliberate, his eyes steady and remorseless.

"Sit down, Mr. Senob," he said hollowly. "I have a message from the lawyers, and I presume I am welcoming to this establishment the new proprietor who has taken the place of my revered chief, whom I have faithfully served for twenty-nine years."

Bones closed his eyes and listened as to an address of welcome.

"Personally," said Mr. Hilton, "I think that the sale of this business is a great mistake on the part of the Siker family. The Sikers have been detectives for four generations," he said with a relish of an antiquarian. "George Siker first started work as an investigator in 1814 in this identical building. For thirty-five years he conducted Siker's Confidential Bureau, and was succeeded by his son James the grandfather of the late John George for twenty-three years——"

"Quite so, quite so," said Bones. "Poor old George! Well, well, we can't live for ever, dear old chief of staff. Now, the thing is, how to improve this jolly old business."

He looked around the dingy apartment without enthusiasm.

Bones had visitors that morning, many visitors. They were not, as he had anticipated, veiled ladies or cloaked dukes, nor did they pour into his discreet ears the stories of misspent lives.

There was Mr. Carlo Borker, of Borker's Confidential Enquiry Bureau, a gross man in a top hat, who complained bitterly that old man Siker had practically and to all intents and purposes offered him an option of the business years ago.

It was a one-sided conversation.

"I says to him: 'Siker, if you ever want to sell out' . . . He says to me: 'Borker, my boy, you've only to offer me a reasonable figure' . . . I says to him: 'Now, Siker, don't ever let anybody else get this business. . .'"

Then there was ex-Inspector Stellingworth, of Stellingworth's Detective Corps, a gloomy man, who painted in the blackest colours the difficulties and tragedies of private investigation, yet seemed willing enough to assume the burden of Siker's Agency, and give Bones a thousand pounds profit on his transaction.

Mr. Augustus Tibbetts spent three deliciously happy days in reorganising the business. He purchased from the local gunsmith a number of handcuffs, which were festooned upon the wall behind his desk and secured secretly—since he did not think that the melancholy Mr. Hilton would approve—a large cardboard box filled to the brim with adjustable beards of every conceivable hue, from bright scarlet to mouse colour.

He found time to relate to a sceptical Hamilton something of his achievements.

"Wonderful case to-day, dear old boy," he said enthusiastically on the third evening. "A naughty old lady has been flirting with a very, very naughty old officer. Husband tremendously annoyed. How that man loves that woman!"

"Which man?" said Hamilton cynically.

"I refer to my client," said Bones not without dignity.

"Look here, Bones," said Hamilton with great seriousness, "do you think this is a very nice business you are in? Personally, I think it's immoral."

"What do you mean—immoral?" demanded the indignant Bones.

"Prying into other people's lives," said Hamilton.

"Lives," retorted the oracular Bones, "are meant to be pried into, dear old thing. An examination of jolly old motives is essential to scientific progress. I feel I am doing a public duty," he went on virtuously, "exposing the naughty, chastising the sinful, and all that sort of thing."

"But, honestly," said Hamilton persistently, "do you think it's the game to chase around collecting purely private details about people's goings on?"

"Certainly," said Bones firmly, "certainly, dear old thing. It's a public duty. Never let it be written on the fair pages of Thiggumy that a Tibbetts shrank back when the call of patriotism—all that sort of thing—you know what I mean?"

"I don't," said Hamilton.

"Well, you're a jolly old dense one," said Bones. "And let me say here and now"—he rammed his bony knuckles on the table and withdrew them with an "Ouch!" to suck away the pain—"let me tell you that, as the Latin poet said, *'Ad What's-his name, ad Thiggumy.'* 'Everything human's frightfully interesting'!"

Bones turned up at his detective office the next morning, full of zeal, and Hilton immediately joined him in his private office.

"Well, we finish one case to-day, I think," said Hilton with satisfaction. "It has been very hard trailing him, but I got a good man on the job, and here's the record."

He held in his hand a sheaf of papers.

"Very good," said Bones. "Excellent! I hope we shall bring the malefactor to justice."

"He's not exactly a malefactor," demurred Hilton. "It is a job we were doing for one of our best clients."

"Excellent, excellent!" murmured Bones. "And well we've done it, I'm sure." He leant back in his chair and half closed his eyes. "Tell me what you have discovered."

"This man's a bit of a fool in some ways," said Hilton.

"Which man—the client?"

"No, the fellow we've been trailing."

"Yes, yes," said Bones. "Go on."

"In fact, I wonder that Mr. de Vinne bothered about him."

"De Vinne?" said Bones sitting up. "Harold de Vinne, the moneyed one?"

"That's him. He's one of our oldest customers," said Hilton.

"Indeed," said Bones, this time without any enthusiasm at all.

"You see, a man did him in the eye," explained Mr. Hilton, "swindled him, and all that sort of thing. Well, I think we have got enough to make this chap look silly."

"Oh, yes," said Bones politely. "What have you got?"

"Well, it appears," said Hilton, "that this chap is madly in love with his typist."

"Which chap?" said Bones.

"The fellow who did Mr. de Vinne in the eye," replied the patient Mr. Hilton. "He used to be an officer on the West Coast of Africa, and was known as Bones. His real name is Tibbetts."

"Oh yes," said Bones.

"Well, we've found out all about him," continued Hilton. "He's got a flat in Jermyn Street, and this girl of his, this typist girl, dines with him. She's not a bad-looking girl, mind you."

Bones rose to his feet, and there was in his face a terrible look.

"Hilton," he said, "do you mean that you have been shadowing a perfectly innocent man and a charming, lovely old typewriter, that couldn't say 'Goo' to a boose?"

Bones was pardonably agitated.

"Do you mean to tell me that this office descends to this low practice of prying into the private lives of virtuous gentlemen and typewriters? Shame upon you, Hilton!" His voice shook. "Give me that report!" He thrust the report into the fire. "Now call up Mr. Borker, and tell him I want to see him on business, and don't disturb me, because I am writing a letter."

He pulled a sheet of paper from his stationery rack and wrote furiously. He hardly stopped to think, he scarcely stopped to spell. His letter was addressed to Mr. de Vinne, and when, on the following day, Mr. Borker took over the business of Siker's Agency, that eminent firm of investigators had one client the less.

Chapter 8

A COMPETENT JUDGE OF POETRY

There were times when Mr. Cresta Morris was called by that name; there were other moments when he was "Mr. Staleyborn." His wife, a placid and trusting woman, responded to either name, having implicit faith in the many explanations which her husband offered to her, the favourite amongst them being that business men were seldom known by the names they were born with.

Thus the eminent firm of drapers Messrs. Lavender & Rosemary were—or was—in private life one Isadore Ruhl, and everybody knew that the maker of Morgan's Superfatted Soap—"the soap with foam"—was a certain member of the House of Lords whose name was not Morgan.

Mrs. Staleyborn, or Morris, had a daughter who ran away from home and became the secretary to Augustus Tibbetts, Managing Director of Schemes Limited, and there were odd moments of the day when Mrs. Staleyborn felt vaguely uneasy about her child's future. She had often, indeed, shed tears between five o'clock in the afternoon and seven o'clock in the evening, which as everybody knows, is the most depressing time of the day.

She was, however, one of those persons who are immensely comforted by the repetition of ancient saws which become almost original every time they are applied, and one of these sayings was "Everything is for the best." She believed in miracles, and had reason, for she received her weekly allowance from her erratic husband with monotonous regularity every Saturday morning.

This is a mere digression to point the fact that Mr. Morris was known by many names. He was called "Cress," and "Ike," and "Tubby," and "Staley," according to the company in which he found himself.

One evening in June he found himself in the society of friends who called him by names which, if they were not strictly original, were certainly picturesque. One of these companions was a Mr. Webber, who had worked more swindles with Morris than had any other partner, and the third, and most talkative, was a gentleman named Seepidge, of Seepidge & Soomes, printers to the trade.

Mr. Seepidge was a man of forty-five, with a well-used face. It was one of those faces which look different from any other angle than that from which it is originally seen. It may be said, too, that his colouring was various. As he addressed Mr. Morris, it varied between purple and blue. Mrs. Morris was in the habit of addressing her husband by endearing titles. Mr. Seepidge was not addressing Mr. Morris in a way which, by any stretch of imagination, could be described as endearing.

"Wait a bit, Lew," pleaded Mr. Morris. "Don't let's quarrel. Accidents will occur in the best of regulated families."

"Which you're not," said the explosive Mr. Seepidge, violently. "I gave you two hundred to back Morning Glory in the three o'clock race. You go down to Newbury with my money, and you come back and tell me, after the horse has won, that you couldn't get a bookmaker to take the bet!"

"And I give you the money back," replied Mr. Morris.

"You did," reported Mr. Seepidge meaningly, "and I was surprised to find there wasn't a dud note in the parcel. No, Ike, you double-crossed me. You backed the horse and took the winnings, and come back to me with a cock-and-bull story about not being able to find a bookmaker."

Mr. Morris turned a pained face to his companion.

"Jim," he said, addressing Mr. Webber, "did you ever in all your born days hear a pal put it across another pal like that? After the work we've done all these years together, me and Lew—why, you're like a serpent in the bush, you are really!"

It was a long time, and there was much passing of glasses across a lead-covered bar, before Mr. Seepidge could be pacified—the meeting took place in the private bar of "The Bread and Cheese," Camden Town—but presently he turned from the reproachful into the melancholy stage, explained the bad condition of business, what with the paper bills and wages bills he had to pay, and hinted ominously at bankruptcy.

In truth, the firm of Seepidge was in a bad way. The police had recently raided the premises and nipped in the bud a very promising order for five hundred thousand sweepstake tickets, which were being printed surreptitiously, for Mr. Secpidge dealt in what is colloquially known as "snide printing."

Whether Mr. Cresta Morris had indeed swindled his partner of many crimes, and had backed Morning Glory at a remunerative price for his own profit, is a painful question which need not be too closely examined. It is certain that Seepidge was in a bad way, and as

Mr. Morris told himself with admirable philosophy, even if he had won a packet of money, a thousand or so would not have been sufficient to get Mr. Seepidge out of the cart.

"Something has got to be done," said Mr. Cresta Morris briskly.

"Somebody," corrected the taciturn Webber. "The question is, who?"

"I tell you, boys, I'm in a pretty bad way," said Seepidge earnestly. "I don't think, even if I'd backed that winner, I could have got out of trouble. The business is practically in pawn; I'm getting a police inspection once a week. I've got a job now which may save my bacon, if I can dodge the 'splits'—an order for a million leaflets for a Hamburg lottery house. And I want the money—bad! I owe about three thousand pounds."

"I know where there's money for asking," said Webber, and they looked at him.

His interesting disclosure was not to follow immediately, for they had reached closing-time, and were respectfully ushered into the street.

"Come over to my club," said Mr. Seepidge.

His club was off the Tottenham Court Road, and its membership was artistic. It had changed its name after every raid that had been made upon it, and the fact that the people arrested had described themselves as artists and actresses consolidated the New Napoli Club as one of the artistic institutions of London.

"Now, where's this money?" asked Seepidge, when they were seated round a little table.

"There's a fellow called Bones——" began Mr. Webber.

"Oh, him!" interrupted Mr. Morris, in disgust. "Good Heavens! You're not going to try him again!"

"We'd have got him before if you hadn't been so clever," said Webber. "I tell you, he's rolling in money. He's just moved into a new flat in Devonshire Street that can't cost him less than six hundred a year."

"How do you know this?" asked the interested Morris.

"Well," confessed Webber, without embarrassment, "I've been working solo on him, and I thought I'd be able to pull the job off myself."

"That's a bit selfish," reproached Morris, shaking his head. "I didn't expect this from you, Webbie."

"Never mind what you expected," said Webber, unperturbed. "I tell you I tried it. I've been nosing round his place, getting information from his servants, and I've learned a lot about him. Mind you," said Mr. Webber, "I'm not quite certain how to use what I know to make money. If I'd known that, I shouldn't have told you two chaps anything about it. But I've got an idea that this chap Bones is a bit sensitive on a certain matter, and Cully Tring, who's forgotten more about human men than I ever knew, told me that, if you can get a mug on his sensitive spot, you can bleed him to death. Now, three heads are better than one, and I think, if we get together, we'll lift enough stuff from Mr. Blinking Bones to keep us at Monte Carlo for six months."

"Then," said Mr. Seepidge impressively, "let us put our 'eads together."

In emotional moments that enterprising printer was apt to overlook the box where the little "h's" were kept.

Bones had indeed moved into the intellectual atmosphere of Devonshire Street. He had hired a flat of great beauty and magnificence, with lofty rooms and distempered walls and marble chimney-pieces, for all the world like those rooms in the catalogues of furniture dealers which so admirably show off the fifty-pound drawing-room suite offered on the easiest terms.

"My dear old thing," he said, describing his new splendours to Hamilton, "you ought to see the jolly old bathroom!"

"What do you want a bath for?" asked Hamilton innocently. "You've only got the place for three years."

"Now, dear old thing, don't be humorous," said Bones severely. "Don't be cheap, dear old comic one."

"The question is," said Hamilton, "why the dickens do you want a new flat? Your old flat was quite a palatial establishment. Are you thinking of setting up housekeeping?"

Bones turned very red. In his embarrassment he stood first upon one leg and then the other, lifting his eyebrows almost to the roof of his head to let in his monocle, and lifted them as violently to let it out again.

"Don't pry, don't pry, dear old Ham," he said testily. "Great Heavens and Moses! Can't a fellow take a desirable flat, with all modern conveniences, in the most fashionable part of the West End, and all that sort of thing, without exciting the voice of scandal, dear old thing? I'm surprised at you, really I am, Ham. I am, Ham," he repeated. "That sounds good," he said, brightening up. "Am Ham!"

"But what is the scheme?" persisted Hamilton.

"A bargain, a bargain, dear old officer," said Bones, hurriedly, and proceeded to the next business.

That next business included the rejection of several very promising offers which had arrived from different directors of companies, and people. Bones was known as a financier. People who wanted other people to put money into things invariably left Bones to the last, because they liked trying the hard things first. The inventor and patentee of the reaping machine that could be worked by the farmer in his study, by means of push keys, was sure, sooner or later, to meet a man who scratched his chin and said:

"Hard luck, but why don't you try that man Tibbetts? He's got an office somewhere around. You'll find it in the telephone book. He's got more money than he knows what to do with, and your invention is the very thing he'd finance."

As a rule, it was the very thing that Bones did not finance.

Companies that required ten thousand pounds for the extension of their premises, and the fulfilment of the orders which were certain to come next year, drafted through their secretaries the most wonderful letters, offering Bones a seat on their board, or even two seats, in exchange for his autograph on the south-east corner of a cheque. These letters usually began somehow like this:

"At a moment when the eyes of the world are turned upon Great Britain, and when her commercial supremacy is threatened, it behoves us all to increase production. . ." And usually there was some reference to "the patriotic duty of capital."

There was a time when these appeals to his better nature would have moved Bones to amazing extravagance, but happily that time was before he had any money to speak about.

For Bones was growing in wisdom and in wiliness as the days passed. Going through the pile of correspondence, he came upon a letter which he read thoughtfully, and then read again before he reached to the telephone and called a number. In the City of London there was a business-like agency which supplied him with a great deal of useful information, and it was to these gentlemen that he addressed his query: "Who are Messrs. Seepidge & Soomes?"

He waited for some time with the receiver at his ear, a far-away look in his eyes, and then the reply came:

"A little firm of printers run by a rascal named Seepidge, who has been twice bankrupt and is now insolvent. His firm has been visited by the police for illegal printing several times, and the firm is in such a low condition that it has a job to pay its wages bill."

"Thank you," said Bones. "Thank you, dear old commercial guardian. What is the business worth?"

"It's worth your while to keep away from it," said the humorous reply, and Bones hung up the receiver.

"Ham, old dear," he said, and Hamilton looked up. "Suppose," said Bones, stretching out his legs and fixing his monocle, "suppose, my jolly old accountant and partner, you were offered a business which was worth"—he paused—"which was worth your while keeping away from it—that's a pretty good line, don't you think, old literary critic?"

"A very good line," said Hamilton calmly; "but you have rather a loud-speaking telephone, and I think I have heard the phrase before."

"Oh, have you?" said Bones by no means abashed. "Still, it's a very good line. And suppose you were offered this printing business for fifteen thousand pounds, what would you say?"

"It depends on who was present," said Ham, "and where I was. For example, if I were in the gorgeous drawing-room of your wonderful flat, in the splendid presence of your lovely lady wife to be——"

Bones rose and wagged his finger.

"Is nothing sacred to you, dear old Ham?" he choked. "Are the most tender emotions, dear old thing, which have ever been experienced by any human being——"

"Oh, shut up," said Hamilton, "and let's hear about this financial problem of yours."

Bones was ruffled, and blinked, and it was some time before he could bring himself back to sordid matters of business.

"Well, suppose this jolly old brigand offered you his perfectly beastly business for fifteen thousand pounds, what would you do?"

"Send for the police," said Hamilton.

"Would you now?" said Bones, as if the idea struck him for the first time. "I never have sent for the police you know, and I've had simply terrible offers put up to me."

"Or put it in the waste-paper basket," said Hamilton, and then in surprise: "Why the dickens are you asking all these questions?"

"Why am I asking all these questions?" repeated Bones. "Because, old thing, I have a hump."

Hamilton raised incredulous eyebrows.

"I have what the Americans call a hump."

"A hump?" said Hamilton, puzzled. "Oh, you mean a 'hunch.'"

"Hump or hunch, it's all the same," said Bones airily. "But I've got it."

"What exactly is your hunch?"

"There's something behind this," said Bones, tapping a finger solemnly on the desk. "There's a scheme behind this—there's a swindle—there's a ramp. Nobody imagines for one moment that a man of my reputation could be taken in by a barefaced swindle of this character. I think I have established in the City of London something of a tradition," he said.

"You have," agreed Hamilton. "You're supposed to be the luckiest devil that ever walked up Broad Street."

"I never walk up Broad Street, anyway," said Bones, annoyed. "It is a detestable street, a naughty old street, and I should ride up it—or, at least, I shall in a day or two."

"Buying a car?" asked Hamilton, interested.

"I'll tell you about that later," said Bones evasively, and went on:

"Now, putting two and two together, you know the conclusion I've reached?"

"Four?" suggested Hamilton.

Bones, with a shrug ended the conversation then and there, and carried his correspondence to the outer office, knocking, as was his wont, until his stenographer gave him permission to enter. He shut the door—always a ceremony—behind him and tiptoed toward her.

Marguerite Whitland took her mind from the letter she was writing, and gave her full attention to her employer.

"May I sit down, dear young typewriter?" said Bones humbly.

"Of course you can sit down, or stand up, or do anything you like in the office. Really," she said, with a laugh, "really, Mr. Tibbetts, I don't know whether you're serious sometimes."

"I'm serious all the time, dear old flicker of keyboards," said Bones, seating himself deferentially, and at a respectful distance.

She waited for him to begin, but he was strangely embarrassed even for him.

"Miss Marguerite," he began at last a little huskily, "the jolly old poet is born and not——"

"Oh, have you brought them?" she asked eagerly, and held out her hand. "Do show me, please!"

Bones shook his head.

"No, I have not brought them," he said. "In fact, I can't bring them yet."

She was disappointed, and showed it.

"You've promised me for a week I should see them."

"Awful stuff, awful stuff!" murmured Bones disparagingly. "Simply terrible tripe!"

"Tripe?" she said, puzzled.

"I mean naughty rubbish and all that sort of thing."

"Oh, but I'm sure it's good," she said. "You wouldn't talk about your poems if they weren't good."

"Well," admitted Bones, "I'm not so sure, dear old arbitrator elegantus, to use a Roman expression, I'm not so sure you're not right. One of these days those poems will be given to this wicked old world, and—then you'll see."

"But what are they all about?" she asked for about the twentieth time.

"What are they about?" said Bones slowly and thoughtfully. "They're about one thing and another, but mostly about my—er—friends. Of course a jolly old poet like me, or like any other old fellow, like Shakespeare, if you like—to go from the sublime to the ridiculous—has fits of poetising that mean absolutely nothing. It doesn't follow that if a poet like Browning or me writes fearfully enthusiastically and all that sort of thing about a person. . . No disrespect, you understand, dear old miss."

"Quite," she said, and wondered.

"I take a subject for a verse," said Bones airily, waving his hand toward Throgmorton Street. "A 'bus, a fuss, a tram, a lamb, a hat, a cat, a sunset, a little flower growing on the river's brim, and all that sort of thing—any old subject, dear old miss, that strikes me in the eye—you understand?"

"Of course I understand," she said readily. "A poet's field is universal, and I quite understand that if he writes nice things about his friends he doesn't mean it."

"Oh, but doesn't he?" said Bones truculently. "Oh, doesn't he, indeed? That just shows what a fat lot you know about it, jolly old Miss Marguerite. When I write a poem about a girl——"

"Oh, I see, they're about girls," said she a little coldly.

"About *a* girl," said Bones, this time so pointedly that his confusion was transferred immediately to her.

"Anyway, they don't mean anything," she said bravely.

"My dear young miss"—Bones rose, and his voice trembled as he laid his hand on the typewriter where hers had been a second before—"my dear old miss," he said, jingling with the letters "a" and "e" as though he had originally put out his hand to touch the keyboard, and was in no way surprised and distressed that the little hand which had covered them had been so hastily withdrawn, "I can only tell you——"

"There is your telephone bell," she said hurriedly. "Shall I answer it?" And before Bones could reply she had disappeared.

He went back to his flat that night with his mind made up. He would show her those beautiful verses. He had come to this conclusion many times before, but his heart had failed him. But he was growing reckless now. She should see them—priceless verses, written in a most expensive book, with the monogram "W.M." stamped in gold upon the cover. And as he footed it briskly up Devonshire Street, he recited:

> "O Marguerite, thou lovely flower,
> I think of thee most every hour,
> With eyes of grey and eyes of blue,
> That change with every passing hue,
> Thy lovely fingers beautifully typing,
> How sweet and fragrant is thy writing!

He thought he was reciting to himself, but that was not the case. People turned and watched him, and when he passed the green doorway of Dr. Harkley Bawkley, the eminent brain specialist, they were visibly disappointed.

He did not unlock the rosewood door of his flat, but rang the silver bell.

He preferred this course. Ali, his Coast servant, in his new livery of blue and silver, made the opening of the door something only less picturesque than the opening of Parliament. This intention may not have been unconnected with the fact that there were two or three young ladies, and very young at that, on the landing, waiting for the door of the opposite flat to open.

Ali opened the door. The lower half of him was blue and silver, the upper half was Oxford shirt and braces, for he had been engaged in cleaning the silver.

"What the deuce do you mean by it?" demanded Bones wrathfully. "Haven't I given you a good uniform, you blithering jackass? What the deuce do you mean by opening the door, in front of people, too, dressed like a—a—dashed naughty boy?"

"Silverous forks require lubrication for evening repast," said Ali reproachfully.

Bones stalked on to his study.

It was a lovely study, with a carpet of beautiful blue. It was a study of which a man might be proud. The hangings were of silk, and the suite was also of silk, and also of blue silk. He sat down at his Louis XVI. table, took a virgin pad, and began to write. The inspiration was upon him, and he worked at top speed.

"I saw a litle bird—a litle bird—a litle bird, floating in the sky," he wrote. "Ever so high! Its pretty song came down, down to me, and it sounded like your voice the other afternoon at tea, at tea. And in its flite I remembered the night when you came home to me."

He paused at the last, because Marguerite Whitland had never come home to him, certainly not at night. The proprieties had to be observed, and he changed the last few lines to: "I remember the day when you came away to Margate on the sea, on the sea."

He had not seen his book of poems for a week, but there was a blank page at the end into which the last, and possibly the greatest, might go. He pulled the drawer open. It was empty. There was no mistaking the fact that that had been the drawer in which the poems had reposed, because Bones had a very excellent memory.

He rang the bell and Ali came, his Oxford shirt and braces imperfectly hidden under a jersey which had seen better days.

"Ali"—and this time Bones spoke rapidly and in Coast Arabic—"in this drawer was a beautiful book in which I had written many things."

Ali nodded.

"Master, that I know, for you are a great poet, and I speak your praises whenever I go into the *café*, for Hafiz did not write more beautifully than you."

"What the dooce," spluttered Bones in English, "do you mean by telling people about me—eh, you scoundrel? What the dooce do you mean by it, you naughty old ebony?"

"Master," said Ali "eulogistic speechification creates admiration in common minds."

He was so unruffled, so complacent, that Bones, could only look at him in wonder. There was, too, about Ali Mahomet a queer look of guilty satisfaction, as of one who had been surprised in a good act.

"Master," he said, "it is true that, contrary to modest desires of humble poets, I have offered praises of your literature to unauthorised persons, sojourning in high-class *café* 'King's Arms,' for my evening refreshment. Also desiring to create pleasant pleasure and surprise, your servant from his own emoluments authorised preparation of said poems in real print work."

Bones gasped.

"You were going to get my things printed? Oh, you. . . oh, you. . ."

Ali was by no means distressed.

"To-morrow there shall come to you a beautiful book for the master's surprise and joyousness. I myself will settle account satisfactorily from emoluments accrued."

Bones could only sit down and helplessly wag his head. Presently he grew calmer. It was a kindly thought, after all. Sooner or later those poems of his must be offered to the appreciation of a larger audience. He saw blind Fate working through his servitor's act. The matter had been taken out of his hands now.

"What made you do it, you silly old josser?" he asked.

"Master, one gentleman friend suggested or proffered advice, himself being engaged in printery, possessing machines——"

A horrible thought came into Bones's head.

"What was his name?" he asked.

Ali fumbled in the capacious depths of his trousers pocket and produced a soiled card, which he handed to Bones. Bones read with a groan:

MESSRS. SEEPIDGE & SOOMES,
Printers to the Trade.

Bones fell back in the padded depths of his writing chair.

"Now, you've done it," he said hollowly, and threw the card back again.

It fell behind Ali, and he turned his back on Bones and stooped to pick up the card. It was a target which, in Bones's then agitated condition, he could scarcely be expected to resist.

BONES SPENT A SLEEPLESS NIGHT, and was at the office early. By the first post came the blow he had expected—a bulky envelope bearing on the flap the sign-manual of Messrs. Seepidge & Soomes. The letter which accompanied the proof enclosed merely repeated the offer to sell the business for fifteen thousand pounds.

"This will include," the letter went on, "a great number of uncompleted orders, one of which is for a very charming series of poems which are now in our possession, and a proof-sheet of which we beg to enclose."

Bones read the poems and they somehow didn't look as well in print as they had in manuscript. And, horror of horrors—he went white at the thought—they were unmistakably disrespectful to Miss Marguerite Whitland! They were love poems. They declared Bones's passion in language which was unmistakable. They told of her hair which was beyond compare, of her eyes which rivalled the skies, and of her lips like scarlet strips. Bones bowed his head in his hands, and was in this attitude when the door opened, and Miss Whitland, who had had a perfect night and looked so lovely that her poems became pallid and nauseating caricatures, stepped quietly into the room.

"Aren't you well, Mr. Tibbetts?" she said.

"Oh, quite well," said Bones valiantly. "Very tra-la-la, dear old thing, dear old typewriter, I mean."

"Is that correspondence for me?"

She held out her hand, and Bones hastily thrust Messrs. Seepidge & Soomes's letter, with its enclosure, into his pocket.

"No, no, yes, yes," he said incoherently. "Certainly why not this is a letter dear old thing about a patent medicine I have just taken I am not all I was a few years ago old age is creeping on me and all that sort of stuff shut the door as you go in."

He said this without a comma or a full-stop. He said it so wildly that she was really alarmed.

Hamilton arrived a little later, and to him Bones made full confession.

"Let's see the poems," said Hamilton seriously.

"You won't laugh?" said Bones.

"Don't be an ass. Of course I won't laugh, unless they're supposed to be comic," said Hamilton. And, to do him justice, he did not so much as twitch a lip, though Bones watched his face jealously.

So imperturbable was Hamilton's expression that Bones had courage to demand with a certain smugness:

"Well, old man, not so bad? Of course, they don't come up to Kipling, but I can't say that I'm fearfully keen on Kipling, old thing. That little one about the sunset, I think, is rather a gem."

"I think you're rather a gem," said Hamilton, handing back the proofs. "Bones, you've behaved abominably, writing poetry of that kind and leaving it about. You're going to make this girl the laughing-stock of London."

"Laughing-stock?" snorted the annoyed Bones. "What the dickens do you mean, old thing? I told you there are no comic poems. They're all like that."

"I was afraid they were," said Hamilton. "But poems needn't be comic," he added a little more tactfully, as he saw Bones's colour rising, "they needn't be comic to excite people's amusement. The most solemn and sacred things, the most beautiful thoughts, the most wonderful sentiments, rouse the laughter of the ignorant."

"True, true," agreed Bones graciously. "And I rather fancy that they are a little bit on the most beautiful side, my jolly old graven image. All heart outpourings you understand—but no, you wouldn't understand, my old crochety one. One of these days, as I've remarked before, they will be read by competent judges. . . midnight oil, dear old thing—at least, I have electric light in my flat. They're generally done after dinner."

"After a heavy dinner, I should imagine," said Hamilton with asperity. "What are you going to do about it, Bones?"

Bones scratched his nose.

"I'm blessed if I know," he said.

"Shall I tell you what you must do?" asked Hamilton quietly.

"Certainly, Ham, my wise old counsellor," said the cheerful Bones. "Certainly, by all means, Why not?"

"You must go to Miss Whitland and tell her all about it."

Bones's face fell.

"Good Heavens, no!" he gasped. "Don't be indelicate, Ham! Why, she might never forgive me, dear old thing! Suppose she walked out of the office in a huff? Great Scotland! Great Jehoshaphat! It's too terrible to contemplate!"

"You must tell her," said Hamilton firmly. "It's only fair to the girl to know exactly what is hanging over her."

Bones pleaded, and offered a hundred rapid solutions, none of which were acceptable to the relentless Hamilton.

"I'll tell her myself, if you like," he said. "I could explain that they're just the sort of things that a silly ass of a man does, and that they were not intended to be offensive—even that one about her lips being like two red strips. Strips of what—carpet?"

"Don't analyse it, Ham, lad, don't analyse it!" begged Bones. "Poems are like pictures, old friend. You want to stand at a distance to see them."

"Personally I suffer from astigmatism," said Hamilton, and read the poems again. He stopped once or twice to ask such pointed questions as how many "y's" were in "skies," and Bones stood on alternate feet, protesting incoherently.

"They're not bad, old boy?" he asked anxiously at last. "You wouldn't say they were bad?"

"Bad," said Hamilton in truth, "is not the word I should apply."

Bones cheered up.

"That's what I think, dear ex-officer," he smirked. "Of course, a fellow is naturally shy about maiden efforts, and all that sort of thing, but, hang it all, I've seen worse than that last poem, old thing."

"So have I," admitted Hamilton, mechanically turning back to the first poem.

"After all"—Bones was rapidly becoming philosophical—"I'm not so sure that it isn't the best thing that could happen. Let 'em print 'em! Hey? What do you say? Put that one about young Miss Marguerite being like a pearl discovered in a dustbin, dear Ham, put it before a competent judge, and what would he say?"

"Ten years," snarled Hamilton, "and you'd get off lightly!"

Bones smiled with admirable toleration, and there the matter ended for the moment.

It was a case of blackmail, as Hamilton had pointed out, but, as the day proceeded, Bones took a more and more lenient view of his enemy's fault. By the afternoon he was cheerful, even jocose, and, even in such moments as he found himself alone with the girl, brought the conversation round to the subject of poetry as one of the fine arts, and cunningly excited her curiosity.

"There is so much bad poetry in the world," said the girl on one such occasion, "that I think there should be a lethal chamber for people who write it."

"Agreed, dear old tick-tack," assented Bones, with an amused smile. "What is wanted is—well, I know, dear old miss. It may surprise you to learn that I once took a correspondence course in poetry writing."

"Nothing surprises me about you, Mr. Tibbetts," she laughed.

He went into her office before leaving that night. Hamilton, with a gloomy shake of his head by way of farewell, had already departed, and Bones, who had given the matter very considerable thought, decided that this was a favourable occasion to inform her of the amusing efforts of his printer correspondent to extract money.

The girl had finished her work, her typewriter was covered, and she was wearing her hat and coat. But she sat before her desk, a frown on her pretty face and an evening newspaper in her hand, and Bones's heart momentarily sank. Suppose the poems had been given to the world?

"All the winners, dear old miss?" he asked, with spurious gaiety.

She looked up with a start.

"No," she said. "I'm rather worried, Mr. Tibbetts. A friend of my step-father's has got into trouble again, and I'm anxious lest my mother should have any trouble."

"Dear, dear!" said the sympathetic Bones. "How disgustingly annoying! Who's the dear old friend?"

"A man named Seepidge," said the girl, and Bones gripped a chair for support. "The police have found that he is printing something illegal. I don't quite understand it all, but the things they were printing were invitations to a German lottery."

"Very naughty, very unpatriotic," murmured the palpitating Bones, and then the girl laughed.

"It has its funny side," she said. "Mr. Seepidge pretended that he was carrying out a legitimate order—a book of poems. Isn't that absurd?"

"Ha, ha!" said Bones hollowly.

"Listen," said the girl, and read:

"'The magistrate, in sentencing Seepidge to six months' hard labour, said that there was no doubt that the man had been carrying on an illegal business. He had had the effrontery to pretend that he was printing a volume of verse. The court had heard extracts from that precious volume, which had evidently been written by Mr. Seepidge's office-boy. He had never read such appalling drivel in his life. He ordered the confiscated lottery prospectuses to be destroyed, and he thought he would be rendering a service to humanity if he added an order for the destruction of this collection of doggerel.'"

The girl looked up at Bones.

"It is curious that we should have been talking about poetry to-day, isn't it?" she asked. "Now, Mr. Tibbetts, I'm going to insist upon your bringing that book of yours to-morrow."

Bones, very flushed of face, shook his head.

"Dear old disciple," he said huskily, "another time. . . another time. . . poetry should be kept for years. . . like old wine. . ."

"Who said that?" she asked, folding her paper and rising.

"Competent judges," said Bones, with a gulp.

Chapter 9

The Lamp That Never Went Out

"Have you seen her?" asked Bones.

He put this question with such laboured unconcern that Hamilton put down his pen and glared suspiciously at his partner.

"She's rather a beauty," Bones went on, toying with his ivory paperknife. "She has one of those dinky bonnets, dear old thing, that makes you feel awfully braced with life."

Hamilton gasped. He had seen the beautiful Miss Whitland enter the office half an hour before, but he had not noticed her head-dress.

"Her body's dark blue, with teeny red stripes," said Bones dreamily, "and all her fittings are nickel-plated——"

"Stop!" commanded Hamilton hollowly. "To what unhappy woman are you referring in this ribald fashion?"

"Woman!" spluttered the indignant Bones. "I'm talking about my car."

"Your car?"

"My car," said Bones, in the off-handed way that a sudden millionaire might refer to "my earth."

"You've bought a car?"

Bones nodded.

"It's a jolly good 'bus," he said. "I thought of running down to Brighton on Sunday."

Hamilton got up and walked slowly across the room with his hands in his pockets.

"You're thinking of running down to Brighton, are you?" he said. "Is it one of those kind of cars where you have to do your own running?"

Bones, with a good-natured smile, also rose from his desk and walked to the window.

"My car," he said, and waved his hand to the street.

By craning his neck, Hamilton was able to get a view of the patch of roadway immediately in front of the main entrance to the building. And undoubtedly there was a car in waiting—a long, resplendent machine that glittered in the morning sunlight.

"What's the pink cushion on the seat?" asked Hamilton.

"That's not a pink cushion, dear old myoptic," said Bones calmly; "that's my chauffeur—Ali ben Ahmed."

"Good lor!" said the impressed Hamilton. "You've a nerve to drive into the City with a sky-blue Kroo boy."

Bones shrugged his shoulders.

"We attracted a certain amount of attention," he admitted, not without satisfaction.

"Naturally," said Hamilton, going back to his desk. "People thought you were advertising Pill Pellets for Pale Poultry. When did you buy this infernal machine?"

Bones, at his desk, crossed his legs and put his fingers together.

"Negotiations, dear old Ham, have been in progress for a month," he recited. "I have been taking lessons on the quiet, and to-day—proof!" He took out his pocket-book and threw a paper with a lordly air towards his partner. It fell half-way on the floor.

"Don't trouble to get up," said Hamilton. "It's your motor licence. You needn't be able to drive a car to get that."

And then Bones dropped his attitude of insouciance and became a vociferous advertisement for the six-cylinder Carter-Crispley ("the big car that's made like a clock"). He became double pages with illustrations and handbooks and electric signs. He spoke of Carter and of Crispley individually and collectively with enthusiasm, affection, and reverence.

"Oh!" said Hamilton, when he had finished. "It sounds good."

"Sounds good!" scoffed Bones. "Dear old sceptical one, that car. . ."

And so forth.

All excesses being their own punishment, two days later Bones renewed an undesirable acquaintance. In the early days of Schemes, Ltd., Mr. Augustus Tibbetts had purchased a small weekly newspaper called the *Flame*. Apart from the losses he incurred during its short career, the experience was made remarkable by the fact that he became acquainted with Mr. Jelf, a young and immensely self-satisfied man in pince-nez, who habitually spoke uncharitably of bishops, and never referred to members of the Government without causing sensitive people to shudder.

The members of the Government retaliated by never speaking of Jelf at all, so there was probably some purely private feud between them.

Jelf disapproved of everything. He was twenty-four years of age, and he, too, had made the acquaintance of the Hindenburg Line. Naturally Bones thought of Jelf when he purchased the *Flame*.

From the first Bones had run the *Flame* with the object of exposing things. He exposed Germans, Swedes, and Turks—which was safe. He exposed a furniture dealer who had made him pay twice for an article because a receipt was lost, and that cost money. He exposed a man who had been very rude to him in the City. He would have exposed James Jacobus Jelf, only that individual showed such eagerness to expose his own shortcomings, at a guinea a column, that Bones had lost interest.

His stock of personal grievances being exhausted, he had gone in for a general line of exposure which embraced members of the aristocracy and the Stock Exchange.

If Bones did not like a man's face, he exposed him. He had a column headed "What I Want to Know," and signed "Senob." in which such pertinent queries appeared as:

"When will the naughty old lord who owns a sky-blue motor-car, and wears pink spats, realise that his treatment of his tenants is a disgrace to his ancient lineage?"

This was one of James Jacobus Jelf's contributed efforts. It happened on this particular occasion that there was only one lord in England who owned a sky-blue car and blush-rose spats, and it cost Bones two hundred pounds to settle his lordship.

Soon after this, Bones disposed of the paper, and instructed Mr. Jelf not to call again unless he called in an ambulance—an instruction which afterwards filled him with apprehension, since he knew that J. J. J. would charge up the ambulance to the office.

Thus matters stood two days after his car had made its public appearance, and Bones sat confronting the busy pages of his garage bill.

On this day he had had his lunch brought into the office, and he was in a maze of calculation, when there came a knock at the door.

"Come in!" he yelled, and, as there was no answer, walked to the door and opened it.

A young man stood in the doorway—a young man very earnest and very mysterious—none other than James Jacobus Jelf.

"Oh, it's you, is it?" said Bones unfavourably "I thought it was somebody important."

Jelf tiptoed into the room and closed the door securely behind him.

"Old man," he said, in tones little above a whisper, "I've got a fortune for you."

"Dear old libeller, leave it with the lift-man," said Bones. "He has a wife and three children."

Mr. Jelf examined his watch.

"I've got to get away at three o'clock, old man," he said.

"Don't let me keep you, old writer," said Bones with insolent indifference.

Jelf smiled.

"I'd rather not say where I'm going," he volunteered. "It's a scoop, and if it leaked out, there would be the devil to pay."

"Oh!" said Bones, who knew Mr. Jelf well. "I thought it was something like that."

"I'd like to tell you, Tibbetts," said Jelf regretfully, "but you know how particular one has to be when one is dealing with matters affecting the integrity of ministers."

"I know, I know," responded Bones, wilfully dense, "especially huffy old vicars, dear old thing."

"Oh, them!" said Jelf, extending his contempt to the rules which govern the employment of the English language. "I don't worry about those poor funny things. No, I am speaking of a matter—you have heard about G.?" he asked suddenly.

"No," said Bones with truth.

Jelf looked astonished.

"What!" he said incredulously. "You in the heart of things, and don't know about old G.?"

"No, little Mercury, and I don't want to know," said Bones, busying himself with his papers.

"You'll tell me you don't know about L. next," he said, bewildered.

"Language!" protested Bones. "You really mustn't use Sunday words, really you mustn't."

Then Jelf unburdened himself. It appeared that G. had been engaged to L.'s daughter, and the engagement had been broken off. . .

Bones stirred uneasily and looked at his watch.

"Dispense with the jolly old alphabet," he said wearily, "and let us get down to the beastly personalities."

Thereafter Jelf's conversation condensed itself to the limits of a human understanding. "G" stood for Gregory—Felix Gregory; "L" for Lansing, who apparently had no Christian name, nor found such appendage necessary, since he was dead. He had invented a lamp, and that lamp had in some way come into Jelf's possession. He was exploiting the invention on behalf of the inventor's daughter, and had named it—he said this with great deliberation and emphasis—"The Tibbetts-Jelf Motor Lamp."

Bones made a disparaging noise, but was interested.

The Tibbetts-Jelf Lamp was something new in motor lamps. It was a lamp which had all the advantages of the old lamp, plus properties which no lamp had ever had before, and it had none of the disadvantages of any lamp previously introduced, and, in fact, had no disadvantages whatsoever. So Jelf told Bones with great earnestness.

"You know me, Tibbetts," he said. "I never speak about myself, and I'm rather inclined to disparage my own point of view than otherwise."

"I've never noticed that," said Bones.

"You know, anyway," urged Jelf, "that I want to see the bad side of anything I take up."

He explained how he had sat up night after night, endeavouring to discover some drawback to the Tibbetts-Jelf Lamp, and how he had rolled into bed at five in the morning, exhausted by the effort.

"If I could only find one flaw!" he said. "But the ingenious beggar who invented it has not left a single bad point."

He went on to describe the lamp. With the aid of a lead pencil and a piece of Bones's priceless notepaper he sketched the front elevation and discoursed upon rays, especially upon ultra-violet rays.

Apparently this is a disreputable branch of the Ray family. If you could only get an ultra-violet ray as he was sneaking out of the lamp, and hit him violently on the back of the head, you were rendering a service to science and humanity.

This lamp was so fixed that the moment Mr. Ultra V. Ray reached the threshold of freedom he was tripped up, pounced upon, and beaten until he (naturally enough) changed colour!

It was all done by the lens.

Jelf drew a Dutch cheese on the table-cloth to Illustrate the point.

"This light never goes out," said Jelf passionately. "If you lit it to-day, it would be alight to-morrow, and the next day, and so on. All the light-buoys and lighthouses around England will be fitted with this lamp; it will revolutionise navigation."

According to the exploiter, homeward bound mariners would gather together on the poop, or the hoop, or wherever homeward bound manners gathered, and would chant a psalm of praise, in which the line "Heaven bless the Tibbetts-Jelf Lamp" would occur at regular intervals.

And when he had finished his eulogy, and lay back exhausted by his own eloquence, and Bones asked, "But what does it *do*?" Jelf could have killed him.

Under any other circumstances Bones might have dismissed his visitor with a lecture on the futility of attempting to procure money under false pretences. But remember that Bones was the proprietor of a new motor-car, and thought motor-car and dreamed motor-car by day and by night. Even as it was, he was framing a conventional expression of regret that he could not interest himself in outside property, when there dawned upon his mind the splendid possibilities of possessing this accessory, and he wavered.

"Anyway," he said, "it will take a year to make."

Mr. Jelf beamed.

"Wrong!" he cried triumphantly. "Two of the lamps are just finished, and will be ready to-morrow."

Bones hesitated.

"Of course, dear old Jelf," he said, "I should like, as an experiment, to try them on my car."

"On your car?" Jelf stepped back a pace and looked at the other with very flattering interest and admiration. "Not your car! *Have* you a car?"

Bones said he had a car, and explained it at length. He even waxed as enthusiastic about his machine as had Mr. Jelf on the subject of the lamp that never went out. And Jelf agreed with everything that Bones said. Apparently he was personally acquainted with the Carter-Crispley car. He had, so to speak, grown up with it. He knew its good points and none of its bad points. He thought the man who chose a car like that must have genius beyond the ordinary. Bones agreed. Bones had reached the conclusion that he had been mistaken about Jelf, and that possibly age had sobered him (it was nearly six months since he had perpetrated his last libel). They parted the best of friends. He had agreed to attend a demonstration at the workshop early the following morning, and Jelf, who was working on a ten per cent. commission basis, and had already drawn a hundred on account from the vendors, was there to meet him.

In truth it was a noble lamp—very much like other motor lamps, except that the bulb was, or apparently was, embedded in solid glass. Its principal virtue lay in the fact that it carried its own accumulator, which had to be charged weekly, or the lamp forfeited its title.

Mr. Jelf explained, with the adeptness of an expert, how the lamp was controlled from the dashboard, and how splendid it was to have a light which was independent of the engine of the car or of faulty accumulators, and Bones agreed to try the lamp for a week. He did more than this: he half promised to float a company for its manufacture, and gave Mr. Jelf fifty pounds on account of possible royalties and commission, whereupon Mr. Jelf faded from the picture, and from that moment ceased to take the slightest interest in a valuable article which should have been more valuable by reason of the fact that it bore his name.

Three days later Hamilton, walking to business, was overtaken by a beautiful blue Carter-Crispley, ornamented, it seemed from a distance, by two immense bosses of burnished silver. On closer examination they proved to be nothing more remarkable than examples of the Tibbett-Jelf Lamp.

"Yes," said Bones airily, "that's the lamp, dear old thing. Invented in leisure hours by self and Jelf. Step in, and I'll explain."

"Where do I step in," asked Hamilton, wilfully dense—"into the car or into the lamp?"

Bones patiently smiled and waved him with a gesture to a seat by his side. His explanation was disjointed and scarcely informative; for Bones had yet to learn the finesse of driving, and he had a trick of thinking aloud.

"This lamp, old thing," he said, "never goes out—you silly old josser, why did you step in front of me? Goodness gracious! I nearly cut short your naughty old life"—(this to one unhappy pedestrian whom Bones had unexpectedly met on the wrong side of the road)—"never goes out, dear old thing. It's out now, I admit, but it's not in working order—Gosh! That was a narrow escape! Nobody but a skilled driver, old Hamilton, could have missed that lamp-post. It is going to create a sensation; there's nothing like it on the market—whoop!"

He brought the car to a standstill with a jerk and within half an inch of a City policeman who was directing the traffic with his back turned to Bones, blissfully unconscious of the doom which almost overcame him.

"I like driving with you, Bones," said Hamilton, when they reached the office, and he had recovered something of his self-possession. "Next to stalking bushmen in the wild, wild woods, I know of nothing more soothing to the nerves."

"Thank you," said Bones gratefully. "I'm not a bad driver, am I?"

"'Bad' is not the word I should use alone," said Hamilton pointedly.

In view of the comments which followed, he was surprised and pained to receive on the following day an invitation, couched in such terms as left him a little breathless, to spend the Sunday exploiting the beauties of rural England.

"Now, I won't take a 'No,'" said Bones, wagging his bony forefinger. "We'll start at eleven o'clock, dear old Ham, and we'll lunch at what-you-may-call-it, dash along the thingummy road, and heigho! for the beautiful sea-breezes."

"Thanks," said Hamilton curtly. "You may dash anywhere you like, but I'm dashed if I dash with you. I have too high a regard for my life."

"Naughty, naughty!" said Bones, "I've a good mind not to tell you what I was going to say. Let me tell you the rest. Now, suppose," he said mysteriously, "that there's a certain lady—a jolly old girl named Vera—ha—ha!"

Hamilton went red.

"Now, listen, Bones," he said; "we'll not discuss any other person than ourselves."

"What do you say to a day in the country? Suppose you asked Miss Vera——"

"Miss Vera Sackwell," replied Hamilton a little haughtily, "if she is the lady you mean, is certainly a friend of mine, but I have no control over her movements. And let me tell you, Bones, that you annoy me when——"

"Hoity, toity!" said Bones. "Heaven bless my heart and soul! Can't you trust your old Bones? Why practise this deception, old thing? I suppose," he went on reflectively, ignoring the approaching apoplexy of his partner, "I suppose I'm one of the most confided-in persons in London. A gay old father confessor, Ham, lad. Everybody tells me their troubles. Why, the lift-girl told me this morning that she'd had measles twice! Now, out with it, Ham!"

If Hamilton had any tender feeling for Miss Vera Sackwell, he was not disposed to unburden himself at that moment. In some mysterious fashion Bones, for the first time in his life, had succeeded in reducing him to incoherence.

"You're an ass, Bones!" he said angrily and hotly. "You're not only an ass, but an indelicate ass! Just oblige me by shutting up."

Bones closed his eyes, smiled, and put out his hand.

"Whatever doubts I had, dear old Ham," he murmured, "are dispelled. Congratulations!"

That night Hamilton dined with a fair lady. She was fair literally and figuratively, and as he addressed her as Vera, it was probably her name. In the course of the dinner he mentioned Bones and his suggestion. He did not tell all that Bones had said.

The suggestion of a day's motoring was not received unfavourably.

"But he can't drive," wailed Hamilton. "He's only just learnt."

"I want to meet Bones," said the girl, "and I think it a most excellent opportunity."

"But, my dear, suppose the beggar upsets us in a ditch? I really can't risk your life."

"Tell Bones that I accept," she said decisively, and that ended the matter.

The next morning Hamilton broke the news.

"Miss Sackwell thanks you for your invitation, Bones."

"And accepts, of course?" said Bones complacently. "Jolly old Vera."

"And I say, old man," said Hamilton severely, "will you be kind enough to remember not to call this lady Vera until she asks you to?"

"Don't be peevish, old boy, don't be jealous, dear old thing. Brother-officer and all that. Believe me, you can trust your old Bones."

"I'd rather trust the lady's good taste," said Hamilton with some acerbity. "But won't it be a bit lonely for you, Bones?"

"But what do you mean, my Othello?"

"I mean three is a pretty rotten sort of party," said Hamilton. "Couldn't you dig up somebody to go along and make the fourth?"

Bones coughed and was immensely embarrassed.

"Well, dear old athlete," he said unnecessarily loudly, "I was thinking of asking my—er——"

"Your—er—what? I gather it's an er," said Hamilton seriously, "but which er?"

"My old typewriter, frivolous one," said Bones truculently. "Any objection?"

"Of course not," said Hamilton calmly. "Miss Whitland is a most charming girl, and Vera will be delighted to meet her."

Bones choked his gratitude and wrung the other's hand for fully two minutes.

He spent the rest of the week in displaying to Hamilton the frank ambitions of his mind toward Miss Marguerite Whitland. Whenever he had nothing to do—which seemed most of the day—he strolled across to Hamilton's desk and discoursed upon the proper respect which all right-thinking young officers have for old typewriters. By the end of the week Hamilton had the confused impression that the very pretty girl who ministered to the literary needs of his partner, combined the qualities of a maiden aunt with the virtues of a grandmother, and that Bones experienced no other emotion than one of reverential wonder, tinctured with complete indifference.

On the sixty-fourth lecture Hamilton struck.

"Of course, dear old thing," Bones was saying, "to a jolly old brigand like you, who dashes madly down from his mountain lair and takes the first engaging young person who meets his eye——"

Hamilton protested vigorously, but Bones silenced him with a lordly gesture.

"I say, to a jolly old rascal like you it may seem—what is the word?"

"'Inexplicable,' I suppose, is the word you are after," said Hamilton.

"That's the fellow; you took it out of my mouth," said Bones. "It sounds inexplicable that I can be interested in a platonic, fatherly kind of way in the future of a lovely old typewriter."

"It's not inexplicable at all," said Hamilton bluntly. "You're in love with the girl."

"Good gracious Heavens!" gasped Bones, horrified. "Ham, my dear old boy. Dicky Orum, Dicky Orum, old thing!"

Sunday morning brought together four solemn people, two of whom were men, who felt extremely awkward and showed it, and two of whom behaved as though they had known one another all their lives.

Bones, who stood alternately on his various legs, was frankly astounded that the meeting had passed off without any sensational happening. It was an astonishment shared by thousands of men in similar circumstances. A word of admiration for the car from Vera melted him to a condition of hysterical gratitude.

"It's not a bad old 'bus, dear old—Miss Vera," he said, and tut-tutted audibly under his breath at his error. "Not a bad old 'bus at all, dear old—young friend. Now I'll show you the gem of the collection."

"They are big, aren't they?" said Vera, properly impressed by the lamps.

"They never go out," said Bones solemnly. "I assure you I'm looking forward to the return journey with the greatest eagerness—I mean to say, of course, that I'm looking forward to the other journey—I don't mean to say I want the day to finish, and all that sort of rot. In fact, dear old Miss Vera, I think we'd better be starting."

He cranked up and climbed into the driver's seat, and beckoned Marguerite to seat herself by his side. He might have done this without explanation, but Bones never did things without explanation, and he turned back and glared at Hamilton.

"You'd like to be alone, dear old thing, wouldn't you?" he said gruffly. "Don't worry about me, dear old lad. A lot of people say you can see things reflected in the glass screen, but I'm so absorbed in my driving——"

"Get on with it!" snarled Hamilton.

It was, nevertheless, a perfect day, and Bones, to everybody's surprise, his own included, drove perfectly. It had been his secret intention to drive to Brighton; but nobody suspected this plan, or cared very much what his intentions had been, and the car was running smoothly across Salisbury Plain.

When they stopped for afternoon tea, Hamilton did remark that he thought Bones had said something about Brighton, but Bones just smiled. They left Andover that night in the dusk; but long before the light had faded, the light which was sponsored by Mr. Jelf blazed whitely in the lamp that never went out. And when the dark came Bones purred with joy, for this light was a wonderful light. It flooded the road ahead with golden radiance, and illuminated the countryside, so that distant observers speculated upon its origin.

"Well, old thing," said Bones over his shoulder, "what do you think of the lamps?"

"Simply wonderful, Bones," agreed Hamilton. "I've never seen anything so miraculous. I can even see that you're driving with one hand."

Bones brought the other hand up quickly to the wheel and coughed. As for Miss Marguerite Whitland, she laughed softly, but nobody heard her.

They were rushing along a country road tree-shaded and high-hedged, and Bones was singing a little song—when the light went out.

It went out with such extraordinary unexpectedness, without so much as a warning flicker, that he was temporarily blinded, and brought the car to a standstill.

"What's up, Bones?" asked Hamilton.

"The light, dear old thing," said Bones. "I think the jolly old typewriter must have touched the key with her knee."

"Indeed?" said Hamilton politely; and Bones, remembering that the key was well over on his side of the car, coughed, this time fiercely.

He switched the key from left to right, but nothing happened.

"Most extraordinary!" said Bones.

"Most," said Hamilton.

There was a pause.

"I think the road branches off a little way up I'll get down and see which is the right road to take," said Bones with sudden cheerfulness. "I remember seeing the old signpost before the—er—lamp went out. Perhaps, Miss Marguerite, you'd like to go for a little walk."

Miss Marguerite Whitland said she thought she would, and they went off together to investigate, leaving Hamilton to speculate upon the likelihood of their getting home that night.

Bones walked ahead with Marguerite, and instinctively their hands sought and found one another. They discovered the cross-roads, but Bones did not trouble to light his match. His heart was beating with extraordinary violence, his lips were dry, he found much difficulty in speaking at all.

"Miss Marguerite," he said huskily, "don't think I'm an awful outsider and a perfect rotter, dear old typewriter."

"Of course I don't," she said a little faintly for Bones's arm was about her.

"Don't think," said Bones, his voice trembling, "that I am a naughty old philanderer; but somehow, dear old miss, being alone with you, and all that sort of stuff——"

And he bent and kissed her, and at that moment the light that never went out came on again with extraordinary fierceness, as though to make up for its temporary absence without leave.

And these two young people were focused as in a limelight, and were not only visible from the car, but visible for miles around.

"Dear me!" said Bones.

The girl said nothing. She shaded her eyes from the light as she walked back. As for Bones, he climbed into the driver's seat with the deliberation of an old gentleman selecting a penny chair in the park, and said, without turning his head:

"It's the road to the left."

"I'm glad," said Hamilton, and made no comment even when Bones took the road to the right.

They had gone a quarter of a mile along this highway when the lamp went out. It went out with as unexpected and startling suddenness as before. Bones jingled the key, then turned.

"You wouldn't like to get out, dear old Ham, and have a look round, would you?"

"No, Bones," said Hamilton drily. "We're quite comfortable."

"You wouldn't like to get down, my jolly old typewriter?"

"No, thank you," said Miss Marguerite Whitland with decision.

"Oh!" said Bones. "Then, under the circumstances, dear old person, we'd all better sit here until——"

At that moment the light came on. It flooded the white road, and the white road was an excellent wind-screen against which the bending head of Bones was thrown into sharp relief.

The car moved on. At regular intervals the light that never went out forsook its home-loving habits and took a constitutional. The occupants of the ear came to regard its eccentricities with philosophy, even though it began to rain, and there was no hood.

On the outskirts of Guildford, Bones was pulled up by a policeman, who took his name because the lights were too bright. On the other side of Guildford he was pulled up by another policeman because he had no light at all. Passing through Kingston, the lamp began to flicker, sending forth brilliant dots and dashes, which continued until they were on Putney Common, where the lamp's message was answered from a camp of Boy Scouts, one signalman of the troop being dragged from his bed for the purpose, the innocent child standing in his shirt at the call of duty.

"A delightful day," said Hamilton at parting that night. (It was nearly twelve o'clock.) "I'm sorry you've had so much trouble with that lamp, Bones. What did you call it?"

"I say, old fellow," said Bones, ignoring the question, "I hope, when you saw me picking a spider off dear old Miss Marguerite's shoulder, you didn't—er—think anything?"

"The only thing I thought was," said Hamilton, "that I didn't see the spider."

"Don't stickle, dear old partner," said Bones testily. "It may have been an earwig. Now, as a man of the world, dear old *blasé* one, do you think I'd compromise an innocent typewriter? Do you think I ought to——" He paused, but his voice was eager.

"That," said Hamilton, "is purely a question for the lady. Now, what are you going to do with this lamp. Are you going to float it?"

Bones scowled at the glaring headlight.

"That depends whether the naughty old things float, Ham," he said venomously. "If you think they will, my old eye-witness, how about tyin' a couple of bricks round 'em before I chuck 'em in. What?"

Chapter 10

The Branch Line

Not all the investments of Bones paid dividends. Some cost him money. Some cost him time. Some—and they were few—cost him both.

Somewhere in a marine store in London lie the battered wrecks of what were once electro-plated motor-lamps of a peculiar and, to Bones, sinister design. They were all that was left of a great commercial scheme, based upon the flotation of a lamp that never went out.

On a day of crisis in Bones's life they had gone out, which was bad. They had come on at an inconvenient moment, which was worse, since they had revealed him and his secretary in tender attitudes. And Bones had gone gaily to right the wrong, and had been received with cold politeness by the lady concerned.

There was a week of gloom, when Bones adopted towards his invaluable assistant the air and manner of one who was in the last stages of a wasting disease. Miss Marguerite Whitland never came into Bones's office without finding him sitting at his desk with his head in his hands, except once, when she came in without knocking and Bones hadn't the time to strike that picturesque attitude.

Indeed, throughout that week she never saw him but he was swaying, or standing with his hand before his eyes, or clutching on to the edge of a chair, or walking with feeble footsteps; and she never spoke to him but he replied with a tired, wan smile, until she became seriously alarmed, thinking his brain was affected, and consulted Captain Hamilton, his partner.

"Look here, Bones, you miserable devil," said Hamilton, "you're scaring that poor girl. What the dickens do you mean by it?"

"Scaring who?" said Bones, obviously pleased. "Am I really? Is she fearfully cut up, dear old thing?"

"She is," said Hamilton truthfully. "She thinks you're going dotty."

"Vulgarity, vulgarity, dear old officer," said Bones, much annoyed.

"I told her you were often like that," Hamilton went on wilfully. "I said that you were a little worse, if anything, after your last love affair——"

"Heavens!" nearly screamed Bones. "You didn't tell her anything about your lovely old sister Patricia?"

"I did not," said Hamilton. "I merely pointed out to her the fact that when you were in love you were not to be distinguished from one whom is the grip of measles."

"Then you're a naughty old fellow," said Bones. "You're a wicked old rascal. I'm surprised at you! Can't a fellow have a little heart trouble——"

"Heart? Bah!" said Hamilton scornfully.

"Heart trouble," repeated Bones sternly. "I've always had a weak heart."

"And a weak head, too," said Hamilton. "Now, just behave yourself, Bones, and stop frightening the lady. I'm perfectly sure she's fond of you—in a motherly kind of way," he added, as he saw Bones's face light up. "And, really, she is such an excellent typist that it would be a sin and a shame to frighten her from the office."

This possibility had not occurred to Bones, and it is likely it had more effect than any other argument which Hamilton could use. That day he began to take an interest in life, stepped gaily into the office and as blithely into his secretary's room. He even made jokes, and dared invite her to tea—an invitation which was declined so curtly that Bones decided that tea was an unnecessary meal, and cut it out forthwith.

All this time the business of Schemes Limited was going forward, if not by leaps and bounds, yet by steady progression. Perhaps it was the restraining influence that Hamilton exercised which prevented the leaps being too pronounced and kept the bounds within bounds, so to speak. It was Schemes Limited which bought the theatrical property of the late Mr. Liggeinstein and re-sold those theatres in forty-eight hours at a handsome profit. It was Bones who did the buying, and it was Hamilton who did the selling—in this case, to the intense annoyance of Bones, who had sat up the greater part of one night writing a four-act play in blank verse, and arriving at the office late, had discovered that his chance of acting as his own producer had passed for ever.

"And I'd written a most wonderful part for you, dear old mademoiselle," he said sadly to his secretary. "The part where you die in the third act—well, really, it brought tears to my jolly old eyes."

"I think Captain Hamilton was very wise to accept the offer of the Colydrome Syndicate," said the girl coldly.

In his leisure moments Bones had other relaxations than the writing of poetry—now never mentioned—or four-act tragedies. What Hamilton had said of him was true. He had an extraordinary nose for a bargain, and found his profits in unexpected places.

People got to know him—quite important people, men who handled millions carelessly, like Julius Bohea, and Important Persons whose faces are familiar to the people of Britain, such as the Right Hon. George Parkinson Chenney. Bones met that most influential member of the Cabinet at a very superior dinner-party, where everybody ate plovers' eggs as though it were a usual everyday occurrence.

And Mr. Parkinson Chenney talked on his favourite subject with great ease and charm, and his favourite subject was the question of the Chinese Concession. Apparently everybody had got concessions in China except the British, until one of our cleverest diplomatists stepped in and procured for us the most amazingly rich coalfield of Wei-hai-tai. The genius and foresight of this diplomatist—who had actually gone to China in the Long Vacation, and of his own initiative and out of his own head had evolved these concessions, which were soon to be ratified by a special commission which was coming from China—was a theme on which Mr. Parkinson Chenney spoke with the greatest eloquence. And everybody listened respectfully, because he was a great man.

"It is not for me," said Mr. Parkinson Chenney, toying with the stem of his champagne glass and closing his eyes modestly, "I say it is not for me—thank you, Perkins, I will have just as much as will come up to the brim; thank you, that will do very nicely—to speak boastfully or to enlarge unduly upon what I regard as a patriotic effort, and one which every citizen of these islands would in the circumstances have made, but I certainly plume myself upon the acumen and knowledge of the situation which I showed."

"Hear, hear!" said Bones in the pause that followed, and Mr. Parkinson Chenney beamed.

When the dinner was over, and the guests retired to the smoking-room, Bones buttonholed the minister.

"Dear old right honourable," said Bones, "may I just have a few words in *re* Chinese coal?"

The right honourable gentleman listened, or appeared to listen. Then Mr. Parkinson Chenney smiled a recognition to another great man, and moved off, leaving Bones talking.

Bones that night was the guest of a Mr. Harold Pyeburt, a City acquaintance—almost, it seemed, a disinterested City acquaintance. When Bones joined his host, Mr. Pyeburt patted him on the back.

"My dear Tibbetts," he said in admiration, "you've made a hit with Chenney. What the dickens did you talk about?"

"Oh, coal," said Bones vaguely.

He wasn't quite certain what he had talked about, only he knew that in his mind at dinner there had dawned a great idea. Was Mr. Pyeburt a thought-reader? Possibly he was. Or possibly some chance word of his had planted the seed which was now germinating so favourably.

"Chenney is a man to know," he said. "He's one of the most powerful fellows in the Cabinet. Get right with him, and you can have a knighthood for the asking."

Bones blushed.

"A knighthood, dear old broker's man?" he said, with an elaborate shrug. "No use to me, my rare old athlete. Lord Bones—Lord Tibbetts I mean—may sound beastly good, but what good is it, eh? Answer me that."

"Oh, I don't know," said Mr. Pyeburt. "It may be nothing to you, but your wife——"

"Haven't a wife, haven't a wife," said Bones rapidly, "haven't a wife!"

"Oh, well, then," said Mr. Pyeburt, "it isn't an attractive proposition to you, and, after all, you needn't take a knighthood—which, by the way, doesn't carry the title of lordship—unless you want to.

"I've often thought," he said, screwing up his forehead, as though in the process of profound cogitation, "that one of these days some lucky fellow will take the Lynhaven Railway off Chenney's hands and earn his everlasting gratitude."

"Lynhaven? Where's that?" asked Bones. "Is there a railway?"

Mr. Pyeburt nodded.

"Come out on to the balcony, and I'll tell you about it," said Pyeburt; and Bones, who always wanted telling about things, and could no more resist information than a dipsomaniac could refuse drink, followed obediently.

It appeared that Mr. Parkinson Chenney's father was a rich but eccentric man, who had a grudge against a certain popular seaside resort for some obscure reason, and had initiated a movement to found a rival town. So he had started Lynhaven, and had built houses and villas and beautiful assembly rooms; and then, to complete the independence of Lynhaven, he had connected that town with the main traffic line by railway, which he built across eight miles of marshland. By all the rules of the game, no man can create successfully in a spirit of vengeance, and Lynhaven should have been a failure. It was, indeed, a great success, and repaid Mr. Chenney, Senior, handsomely.

But the railway, it seemed, was a failure, because the rival town had certain foreshore rights, and had employed those to lay a tramway from their hustling centre; and as the rival town was on the main line, the majority of visitors preferred going by the foreshore route in preference to the roundabout branch line route, which was somewhat handicapped by the fact that this, too, connected with the branch line at Tolness, a little town which had done great work in the War, but which did not attract the tourist in days of peace.

These were the facts about the Lynhaven line, not as they were set forth by Mr. Pyeburt—who took a much more optimistic view of the possibilities of the railway than did its detractors—but as they really were.

"It's a fine line, beautifully laid and ballasted," said Mr. Pyeburt, shaking his head with melancholy admiration. "All that it wants behind it is a mind. At present it's neglected; the freights and passenger fares are too high, the rolling-stock wants replacing, but the locomotive stock is in most excellent condition."

"Does he want to sell it?" asked the interested Bones, and Mr. Pyeburt pursed his lips.

"It is extremely doubtful," he said carefully, "but I think he might be approached. If he does want to sell it, and you can take it off his hands——"

He raised his own eyebrows with a significant gesture, which expressed in some subtle way that Bones's future was assured.

Bones said he would think the matter over, and he did—aloud, in the presence of Hamilton.

"It's a queer proposition," said Hamilton. "Of course, derelict railways can be made to pay."

"I should be general manager," said Bones more thoughtfully still. "My name would be printed on all the posters, of course. And isn't there a free pass over all the railways for railway managers?"

"I believe there is something of the sort," said Hamilton, "but, on the whole, I think it would be cheaper to pay your fare than to buy a railway to get that privilege."

"There is one locomotive," mused Bones. "It is called 'Mary Louisa.' Pyeburt told me about it just as I was going away. Of course, one would get a bit of a name and all that sort of thing."

He scratched his chin and walked thoughtfully into the office of Miss Marguerite Whitland.

She swung round in her chair and reached for her notebook, but Bones was not in a dictatorial mood.

"Young miss," he asked, "how do you like Sir Augustus?"

"Sir who?" she demanded, puzzled.

"Sir Augustus," repeated Bones.

"I think it's very funny," she said.

It was not the answer he expected, and instinctively she knew she had made a mistake.

"Oh, you're thinking about yourself," she said quickly. "Are you going to be a knight, Mr. Tibbetts? Oh, how splendid!"

"Yes," admitted Bones, with fine indifference, "not bad, dear old miss. I'm pretty young, of course, but Napoleon was a general at twenty-two."

"Are you going back into the Army?" she asked a little hazily, and had visions of Bones at the War Office.

"I'm talking about railways," said Bones firmly. "Sir Augustus Tibbetts—there, now I've said it!"

"Wonderful!" said the girl enthusiastically, and her eyes shone with genuine pleasure. "I didn't see it in the newspaper, or I would have congratulated you before."

Bones shifted uneasily.

"As a matter of fact, dear old miss," he said, "it has not been gazetted yet. I'm merely speaking of the future, dear old impetuous typewriter and future secretary to the Lynhaven Railway Company, and possibly dear old Lady——" He stopped short with one of his audible "tuts."

Happily she could not see the capital "L" to the word "Lady," and missed the significance of Bones's interrupted speech.

HE SAW MR. HAROLD PYEBURT AT his office, and Mr. Harold Pyeburt had seen the Right Hon. Parkinson Chenney, and the right honourable gentleman had expressed his willingness to sell the railway, lock, stock, and barrel, for sixty thousand pounds.

"And I advise you"—Mr. Pyeburt paused, as he thought of a better word than "disinterestedly"—"as a friend, to jump at it. Parkinson Chenney spoke in the highest terms of you. You evidently made a deep impression upon him."

"Who is the jolly old Parkinson's agent?" asked Bones, and Mr. Harold Pyeburt admitted without embarrassment that, as a matter of fact, he was acting as Parkinson's attorney in this matter, and that was why he had been so diffident in recommending the property. The audacity of the latter statement passed unnoticed by Bones.

In the end Bones agreed to pay ten per cent. of the purchase price, the remainder to be paid after a month's working of the line, if the deal was approved.

"Clever idea of mine, dear old Ham," said Bones. "The Honours List will be out in a month, and I can easily chuck it."

"That's about the eighth fellow who's paid a ten per cent. deposit," said Mr. Chenney to his agent. "I'll be almost sorry if he takes it."

Three weeks later there were two important happenings. The Prime Minister of England, within an hour of leaving for the West of England to take a well-earned rest, summoned to him his right-hand man.

"Chenney," he said, "I really must go away for this rest, and I'm awfully sorry I cannot be on hand to meet the Chinese Commission. Now, whatever you do, you will not fail to meet them at Charing Cross on their arrival from the Continent. I believe they are leaving Paris to-morrow."

"I shall be there," said Parkinson Chenney, with a little smile. "I rather fancy I have managed their coal concession well, Prime Minister."

"Yes, yes," said the Prime Minister, who was not in the mood for handing out bouquets. "And would you run down to Tolness and settle up that infernal commission of inquiry? They've been asking questions in the House, and I can give no very definite reply. Solebury threatened to force a division when the vote came up. Undoubtedly there's been a great deal of extravagance, but you may be able to wangle a reasonable explanation."

"Trust me, Prime Minister," said Mr. Parkinson Chenney, and left that afternoon by special train for Tolness.

On that very morning Bones, in a pair of overalls and with a rapt expression, stood with his hand on the starting lever of "Mary Louisa," and explained to the secretary of the company—she also wore white overalls and sat in the cab of the engine—just how simple a matter it was to drive a locomotive.

For two glorious days Bones had driven the regular service between Lynhaven and Bayham Junction, where the lines met. He had come to know every twist and turn of the road, every feature of the somewhat featureless landscape, and the four passengers who travelled regularly every day except Sundays—there was no Sunday service—were now so familiar to him that he did not trouble to take their tickets.

The Lynhaven Railway system was not as elaborate as he had thought. He had been impressed by the number of railway trucks which stood in the siding at the terminus, but was to discover that they did not belong to the railway, the rolling stock of which consisted of "Mary Louisa," an asthmatic but once famous locomotive, and four weather-beaten coaches. The remainder of the property consisted of a half right in a bay platform at Bayham Junction and the dilapidated station building at Lynhaven, which was thoughtfully situated about two miles from the town.

Nobody used the railway; that was the stark truth borne in upon Marguerite Whitland. She recognised, with a sense of dismay, the extraordinary badness of the bargain which Bones had made. Bones, with a real locomotive to play with—he had given the aged engine-driver a week's holiday—saw nothing but the wonderful possibilities of pulling levers and making a mass of rusting machinery jerk asthmatically forward at the touch of his hand.

"There are a lot of people," said Bones, affectionately patting a steam pipe, "a lot of people," he said, after sucking his fingers, for the steam was extraordinarily hot, "who think poor old 'Mary Louisa' is done for. Believe me, dear old miss, this locomotive wants a jolly lot of beating, she does really. I haven't tried her full out—have I, jolly old stoker?"

The jolly old stoker, aged seventeen, shook a grimy face.

"And don't you try, neither," he said ominously. "Old George, he never takes her more than quarter speed, he don't."

"Do you hear, dear old miss?" said Bones triumphantly. "Not more than quarter speed. I tell you I could make enough money out of this engine alone to pay the whole cost of the railway.

"What about giving engine-driving lessons? That's an idea! And what about doing wonderful cinema pictures? That's another idea! Thrilling rescues from the train; jolly old hero struggling like mad on the roof of the carriage; railway collisions, and so forth, and so on."

"You can't have a collision unless you've two engines," said the girl.

"Oh, well," said the optimistic Bones, "we could perhaps borrow an engine from the Great Northern."

He looked down at the girl, then looked at his watch.

"Time to be up and doing, dear old thing," he said, and looked back along the little train. The aged guard was sitting on a barrow, his nodding head testifying to the sleep-giving qualities of Lynhaven air. Bones jerked the whistle, there was an unearthly shriek, and the guard woke up. He looked at his watch, yawned, searched the train for passengers, waved his flag, and climbed into his little compartment.

The engine shrieked again. Bones pulled over the lever gently, and there was a gratifying chuck-chuck-chuck. Bones smiled down at the girl.

"Easy as shelling peas, dear old thing," he said, "and this time I'm going to show you just how she can go."

"Old Joe don't let her go more than quarter speed," said the diminutive stoker warningly.

"Blow old Joe!" said Bones severely. "He's a jolly unenterprising old engine-driver. That's why the naughty old line doesn't pay. The idea of running 'Mary Louisa' at quarter speed!"

He turned to the girl for approval, but she felt that, in the circumstances and with only the haziest knowledge of engineering, it would be wiser to offer no opinion.

Bones pushed the lever a little farther over, and the "Mary Louisa" reeled under the shock.

"In *re* knighthood, dear old miss," said Bones confidentially. His words came jerkily, because the footplate of an outraged locomotive pounding forward at an unaccustomed speed was not a good foundation for continued eloquence. "Rendering the jolly old country a service— helping the Cabinet—dear old Chenney awfully fond of me——"

"Aren't we going rather fast?" said the girl, gripping the side of the cab for support.

"Not at all," jerked Bones, "not at all. I am going to show 'em just how this——"

He felt a touch on his arm, and looked down at the diminutive stoker.

"There's a lot of sand round here," said the melancholy child; "it won't hurt you to jump I'm going to."

"Jump!" gasped Bones. "What do you mean? Hey! Don't do that, you silly young——"

But his black-visaged assistant was already poised on the step of the engine, and Bones, looking back, saw him performing somersaults down a sandy slope. Bones looked at the girl in amazement.

"Suicide, dear old miss!" he said in an awed voice. "Terrible!"

"Isn't that a station?" said the girl, more interested for the moment in her own future.

Bones peered through the windows ahead.

"That's the junction, dear old thing," he said. "This is where we stop her."

He tugged at the lever, but the lever was not to be moved. He tugged desperately, but it seemed the steel bar was riveted in position. The "Mary Louisa" was leaping along at an incredible speed, and less than five hundred yards away was the dead-end of the Bayham platform, into which the Lynhaven train was due to run.

Bones went white and looked at the girl with fearful eyes. He took a swift scrutiny to the left and right, but they had passed out of the sandy country, and any attempt to leave the train now would mean certain destruction.

THE RIGHT HONOURABLE MR. PARKINSON CHENNEY had concluded a very satisfactory morning's work of inspection at Tolness, and had secured all the information he needed to answer any question which might be put to him in Parliament by the best-informed of questioners.

He was lunching with the officers of the small garrison, when a telephone message was brought to him. He read it and smiled.

"Good!" he said. "Gentlemen, I am afraid I have to leave you a little earlier than I expected. Colonel Wraggle, will you see that my special train is ready! I must leave in ten minutes. The Chinese Commission has arrived," he said impressively, "or, rather, it arrives in London this afternoon, and I am deputed by the Prime Minister——"

He explained to his respectful audience just what part he had played in securing Chinese Coal Concessions. He made a little speech on the immense value to the Empire in particular and the world in general of these new coalfields which had been secured to the country through the acumen, genius, forethought, and patriotic disinterestedness of the Cabinet.

He would not claim to set any particular merit on his own action, and went on to claim it. By which time his train was ready. It was indeed vital that he should be in London to meet a commission which had shown such reluctance to trade with foreign devils, and had been, moreover, so punctilious in its demand for ceremonious receptions, but he had not the slightest doubt about his ability to reach London before the boat train arrived. He had two and a half hours, and two and a half hours gave him an ample margin of time.

Just before his special rounded the bend which brought it within sight of Bayham Junction the Lynhaven express had reached within a few hundred yards of annihilation. The signalman at Bayham Junction had watched the oncoming rush of Bones's train, and, having a fairly extensive knowledge of the "Mary Louisa" and her eccentricities, he realised just what had happened.

There was only one thing to be done. He could see the smoke from the Cabinet Minister's special rising above the cutting two miles away, and he threw over two levers simultaneously. The first set the points which brought the Lynhaven express on to the main line, switching it from the deadly bay wherein the runaway train would have been smashed to pieces; the second lever set the distant signal against the special. It was a toss-up whether the special had not already passed the distant signal, but he had to take that risk.

Bones, with his arm round the girl, awaiting a noisy and violent dissolution, felt the "Mary Louisa" sway to the right when it should have swayed to the left, heard the clang of the points as he passed them, and drew a long breath when he found himself headed along a straight clear stretch of line. It was some time before he found his voice, and then it was little more than a squeak.

"We're going to London, dear old thing," he said tremulously.

The girl smiled, though her face was deathly pale.

"I thought we were going to heaven," she said.

"Never, dear old thing," said Bones, recovering something of his spirits as he saw the danger past. "Old Bones will never send you there."

The problem of the "Mary Louisa" was still unsettled. She was tearing away like a Flying Dutchman. She was oozing steam at every pore, and, glancing back, Bones saw the agitated countenance of the aged guard thrust through the window. He waved frantically at Bones, and Bones waved genially back again.

He was turning back to make another attempt on the lever, when, looking past the guard, he saw a sight which brought his heart into his mouth. Pounding along behind him, and emitting feathers of steam from her whistle, was an enormous locomotive. Bones guessed there was a train behind it, but the line was too straight for him to see.

"Gracious heavens!" he gasped. "We're being chased!"

He jerked at the lever—though it was a moment when he should have left it severely alone—and to his ill-founded joy it moved.

The two trains came to a standstill together ten miles from Bayham Junction, and Bones climbed down into the six-foot way and walked back.

Almost the first person he met was a gesticulating gentleman in a frock coat and with a red face, who, mistaking him for an engine-driver, dismissed him on the spot, threatened him with imprisonment—with or without hard labour he did not specify—and demanded what the dickens he meant by holding up a Cabinet Minister?

"Why," chortled Bones, "isn't it my dear friend, Mr. Chenney?"

"Who are you," snarled Mr. Chenney, "and what do you mean by calling me your dear friend? By Heavens, I'll have you kicked out of this service!"

"Don't you know old Tibbetts?" cooed Bones. "Well, well, fancy meeting you!"

He held out a grimy hand, which was not taken.

"Tibbetts!" growled the gentleman. "Oh, you are the foo—the gentleman who bought the Lynhaven line, didn't you?"

"Certainly," said Bones.

"But what is your train doing here?" asked Mr. Chenney violently. "Don't you realise you are holding up a special? Great Heavens, man, this is very serious! You are holding up the business of the country!"

The engine-driver of the special came to the rescue.

"There's a switch-over about half a mile further on," he said. "There's not a down train due for an hour. I'll unlock the switch and put you on to the other line, and, after we have passed, you can come on."

"But I don't want to come on, dear old thing," said Bones. "I want to go back."

"Well, that's simple," said the driver.

He it was who piloted the Lynhaven express for another half-mile up the road. He it was who found the switches, unlocked them, telegraphed to the next station to hold up traffic, and he it was—Bones insisted upon this—who brought the "Mary Louisa" along the switch to the down line.

The position was as follows: The "Mary Louisa" was on the down line. Two coaches were between the down and the up line, and the guard's van was exactly on the up line, when the "Mary Louisa" refused to work any further.

Neither the experienced engine-driver, nor Bones, nor the stoker of the special, nor Mr. Chenney, nor the ancient guard, could coax the "Mary Louisa" to move another yard. The Lynhaven express stretched across both lines and made all further progress for traffic impossible.

Three hours later a breakdown gang arrived and towed the "Mary Louisa" and her appendages back to Bayham Junction.

Bones and the girl went back to London by the last train, and Bones was very thoughtful and silent.

But Bones was ever an optimist. The next morning he saw on a newspaper placard: "Birthday Honours. Twenty-two New Knights." And he actually stopped his car, bought a paper, and searched the lists for his name. It was not there.

Chapter 11

A Student of Men

M r. Jackson Hyane was one of those oldish-looking young men to whom the description of "man about town" most naturally applied. He was always well-dressed and correctly dressed. You saw him at first nights. He was to be seen in the paddock at Ascot—it was a shock to discover that he had not the Royal Enclosure badge on the lapel of his coat—and he was to be met with at most of the social functions, attendance at which did not necessarily imply an intimate acquaintance with the leaders of Society, yet left the impression that the attendant was, at any rate, in the swim, and might very well be one of the principal swimmers.

He lived off Albemarle Street in a tiny flat, and did no work of any kind whatever. His friends, especially his new friends, thought he "had a little money," and knew, since he told them, that he had expectations. He did not tell them that his expectations were largely bound up in their credulity and faith in his integrity. Some of them discovered that later, but the majority drifted out of his circle poorer without being wiser, for Mr. Hyane played a wonderful game of piquet, and seemed to be no more than abnormally lucky.

His mother had been a Miss Whitland, his father was the notorious Colonel Hyane, who boasted that his library was papered with High Court writs, and who had had the distinction of being escorted from Monte Carlo by the police of the Principality.

Mr. Jackson Hyane was a student of men and affairs. Very little escaped his keen observation, and he had a trick of pigeon-holing possibilities of profit, and forgetting them until the moment seemed ripe for their exploitation. He was tall and handsome, with a smile which was worth at least five thousand pounds a year to him, for it advertised his boyish innocence and enthusiasm—he who had never been either a boy or enthusiastic.

One grey October day he put away his pass-book into a drawer and locked it, and took from a mental pigeon-hole the materials of an immature scheme. He dressed himself soberly and well, strolled down into Piccadilly, and calling a cab, drove to the block of City buildings which housed the flourishing business of Tibbetts and Hamilton, Limited.

The preliminaries to this invasion had been very carefully settled. He had met Miss Marguerite Whitland by "accident" a week before, had called at her lodgings with an old photograph of her father, which he had providentially discovered, and had secured from her a somewhat reluctant acceptance of an invitation to lunch.

Bones looked up from his desk as the debonair young man strolled in.

"You don't know me, Mr. Tibbetts," said Jackson Hyane, flashing his famous smile. "My name is Hyane."

It was his first meeting with Bones, but by no means the first time that Jackson had seen him.

"My dear old Hyane, sit down," said Bones cheerfully. "What can we do for you?"

Mr. Hyane laughed.

"There's nothing you can do for me, except to spare your secretary for an hour longer than she usually takes."

"My secretary?" said Bones quickly, and shot a suspicious glance at the visitor.

"I mean Miss Whitland," said Hyane easily. "She is my cousin, you know. My mother's brother was her father."

"Oh, yes," said Bones a little stiffly.

He felt a sense of the strongest resentment against the late Professor Whitland. He felt that Marguerite's father had played rather a low trick on him in having a sister at all, and Mr. Hyane was too keen a student to overlook Bones's obvious annoyance.

"Yes," he went on carelessly, "we are quite old friends, Marguerite and I, and you can't imagine how pleased I am that she has such an excellent job as this."

"Oh, yes," said Bones, clearing his throat. "Very nice old—very good typewriter indeed, Mr. Hyane. . . very nice person. . . ahem!"

Marguerite, dressed for the street, came in from her office at that moment, and greeted her cousin with a little nod, which, to the distorted vision of Bones, conveyed the impression of a lifelong friendship.

"I have just been asking Mr. Tibbetts," said Hyane, "if he could spare you for an extra hour."

"I am afraid that can't——" the girl began.

"Nonsense, nonsense!" said Bones, raising his voice as he invariably did when he was agitated. "Certainly, my dear old—er—my dear young—er—certainly, Miss Marguerite, by all means, take your cousin to the Zoo. . . I mean show him the sights."

He was patently agitated, and watched the door close on the two young people with so ferocious a countenance that Hamilton, a silent observer of the scene, could have laughed.

Bones walked slowly back to his desk as Hamilton reached for his hat.

"Come on, Bones," he said briskly. "It's lunch time. I had no idea it was so late."

But Bones shook his head.

"No, thank you, dear old thing," he said sadly. "I'd rather not, if you don't mind."

"Aren't you coming to lunch?" asked Hamilton, astonished.

Bones shook his head.

"No, dear old boy," he said hollowly. "Ask the girl to send me up a stiff glass of soda-water and a biscuit—I don't suppose I shall eat the biscuit."

"Nonsense!" said Hamilton. "Half an hour ago you were telling me you could eat a cart-horse."

"Not now, old Ham," said Bones. "If you've ordered it, send it back. I hate cart-horses, anyway."

"Come along," wheedled Hamilton, dropping his hand on the other's shoulder. "Come and eat. Who was the beautiful boy?"

"Beautiful boy?" laughed Bones bitterly. "A fop, dear old Ham! A tailor's dummy! A jolly old clothes-horse—that's what he was. I simply loathe these people who leap around the City for a funeral. It's not right, dear old thing. It's not manly, dear old sport. What the devil did her father have a sister for? I never knew anything about it."

"They ought to have told you," said Hamilton sympathetically. "Now come and have some food."

But Bones refused. He was adamant. He would sit there and starve. He did not say as much, but he hinted that, when Hamilton returned, his famished and lifeless form would be found lying limply across the desk. Hamilton went out to lunch alone, hurried through his meal, and came back to find Bones alive but unhappy.

He sat making faces at the table, muttering incoherent words, gesticulating at times in the most terrifying manner, and finally threw himself back into his deep chair, his hands thrust into his trousers pockets, the picture of dejection and misery.

It was three o'clock when Miss Marguerite Whitland returned breathless, and, to Bones's jealous eye, unnecessarily agitated.

"Come, come, dear old miss," he said testily. "Bring your book. I wish to dictate an important letter. Enjoyed your lunch?"

The last question was asked in so threatening a tone that the girl almost jumped.

"Yes—no," she said. "Not very much really."

"Ha, ha!" said Bones, insultingly sceptical, and she went red, flounced into her room, and returned, after five minutes, a haughty and distant young woman.

"I don't think I want to dictate, dear old—dear young typewriter," he said unhappily. "Leave me, please."

"Really, my dear Bones," protested Hamilton, when the girl had gone back, scarlet-faced to her office, "you're making a perfect ass of yourself. If a girl cannot go to lunch with her cousin——"

Bones jumped up from his chair, shrugged his shoulders rapidly, and forced a hideous grin.

"What does it matter to me, dear old Ham?" he asked. "Don't think I'm worried about a little thing like a typewriter going out to lunch. Pooh! Absurd! Tommy rot! No, my partner, I don't mind—in fact, I don't care a——"

"Jot," said Hamilton, with the gesture of an outraged bishop.

"Of course not," said Bones wildly. "What does it matter to me? Delighted that young typewriter should have a cousin, and all that sort of thing!"

"Then what the dickens is the matter with you?" asked Hamilton.

"Nothing," said Bones, and laughed more wildly than ever.

Relationships between Mr. Augustus Tibbetts, Managing Director of Schemes Limited, and Miss Marguerite Whitland, his heaven-sent secretary, were strained to the point of breaking that afternoon. She went away that night without saying good-bye, and Bones, in a condition of abject despair, walked home to Devonshire Street, and was within a dozen yards of his flat, when he remembered that he had left his motor-car in the City, and had to take a cab back to fetch it.

"Bones," said Hamilton the next morning, "do you realise the horrible gloom which has come over this office?"

"Gloom, dear old Ham?" said the dark-eyed Bones. He had spent the night writing letters to Marguerite, and had exhausted all the stationery in sight in the process. "Gloom, old thing! Good gracious, no! Nobody is gloomy here!"

"I can tell you somebody who is," said Hamilton grimly. "That unfortunate girl you've been barking at all the morning——"

"Barking at her?" gasped Bones. "Gracious Heavens, I haven't betrayed my worried condition of mind, dear old thing? I thought I hid it rather well."

"What on earth are you worried about?" asked Hamilton, and Bones shrugged.

"Oh, nothing," he said. "Nothing at all. A little fever, dear old thing, contracted in the service of King—God bless him!—and country."

Hamilton's words had this effect, that he brightened visibly, and for the rest of the morning was almost normal. His spirits took a quick downward turn at five minutes to one, when the debonair Mr. Hyane appeared most unexpectedly.

"I'm afraid you'll think I'm a most awful nuisance, Mr. Tibbetts," he said, "but there are so many things which I must really talk to my cousin about—family affairs, you know."

"Don't apologise," said Bones gruffly.

"I shan't keep her beyond the hour," smiled Mr. Hyane. "I realise that you are a very busy man."

Bones said nothing, and when Marguerite Whitland appeared, he had gained sufficient control of his emotions to indulge in a feeble jest. The girl's face was a study at the sight of her cousin. Hamilton, a disinterested observer, read astonishment, annoyance, and resignation in the wide-opened eyes. Bones, who prided himself upon a working knowledge of physiognomy, diagnosed the same symptoms as conveying a deep admiration combined with the re-awakening of a youthful love.

"Hello, Jackson!" she said coldly. "I didn't expect to see you."

"I told you I would call," he smiled. "I must see you, Marguerite, and Mr. Tibbetts has been so kind that I am sure he will not mind me——"

"Mr. Tibbetts is not concerned about the manner in which I spend my lunch hour," she said stiffly, and Bones groaned inwardly.

There was a silence which Hamilton had not the heart to break after the two had gone, and it was Bones who uttered the first comment.

"That's that," he said, and his voice was so quiet and normal that Hamilton stared at him in astonishment.

"Let's have lunch," said Bones briskly, and led the way out.

Not even when Miss Whitland came to him that afternoon and asked for permission to take two days' holiday did his manner change.

With a courtesy entirely free from that extravagance to which she had grown accustomed, he acceded to her request, and she was on the point of explaining to him the reason she had so unexpectedly asked for a vacation, but the memory of his earlier manner checked her.

It was a very simple explanation. Jackson Hyane was a very plausible man. Marguerite Whitland had heard something of her erratic cousin, but certainly nothing in his manner supported the more lurid descriptions of his habits. And Mr. Jackson Hyane had begged her, in the name of their relationships, to take a trip to Aberdeen to examine title-deeds which, he explained, would enable her to join with him in an action of the recovery of valuable Whitland property which was in danger of going to the Crown, and she had consented.

The truth was, there had always been some talk in the family of these estates, though nobody knew better than Jackson Hyane how unsubstantial were the claims of the Whitlands to the title. But the Scottish estate had been docketed away in the pigeon-holes of his mind, and promised to be more useful than he had anticipated.

That afternoon he packed his bag at his flat, put his passport and railway tickets together in his inside pocket, and made his final preparations for departure.

An old crony of his called whilst he was drinking the cup of tea which the housekeeper of the flats had prepared, and took in the situation revealed by the packed suit-cases and the burnt papers in the hearth.

"Hello, Johnny!" he said. "You're getting out, eh?"

Jackson nodded. There was no need to pretend anything with one of his own class.

"Couldn't you square the bank?"

Jackson shook his head.

"No, Billy," he said cheerfully, "I couldn't square it. At this identical moment there are several eminent people in the West End of London who are making applications for warrants."

"Dud cheques, eh?" asked the other thoughtfully. "Well, it had to come, Johnny. You've had a lot of bad luck."

"Atrocious," said Mr. Jackson Hyane. "There's plenty of money in Town, but it's absolutely impossible to get at it. I haven't touched a mug for two months, and I've backed more seconds than I care to think about. Still," he mused, "there's a chance."

His friends nodded. In their circle there was always "a chance," but he could not guess that that chance which the student of men,

Mr. Jackson Hyane, was banking upon answered indifferently to the name of Tibbetts or Bones.

At half-past eight that night he saw his cousin off from King's Cross. He had engaged a sleeper for her, and acted the part of dutiful relative to the life, supplying her with masses of literature to while away the sleepless hours of the journey.

"I feel awfully uncomfortable about going away," said the girl, in a troubled voice. "Mr. Tibbetts would say that he could spare me even if he were up to his eyes in work. And I have an uncomfortable feeling at the back of my mind that there was something I should have told him—and didn't."

"Queer bird, Tibbetts!" said the other curiously. "They call him Bones, don't they?"

"I never do," said the girl quietly; "only his friends have that privilege. He is one of the best men I have ever met."

"Sentimental, quixotic, and all that sort of thing, eh?" said Jackson, and the girl flushed.

"He has never been sentimental with me," she said, but did not deceive the student of men.

When the train had left the station, he drove straightaway to Devonshire Street. Bones was in his study, reading, or pretending to read, and the last person he expected to see that evening was Mr. Jackson Hyane. But the welcome he gave to that most unwelcome visitor betrayed neither his distrust nor his frank dislike of the young well-groomed man in evening-dress who offered him his hand with such a gesture of good fellowship.

"Sit down, Mr.—er——" said Bones.

There was a cold, cold feeling at his heart, a sense of coming disaster, but Bones facing the real shocks and terrors of life was a different young man from the Bones who fussed and fumed over its trifles.

"I suppose you wonder why I have come to see you, Mr. Tibbetts," said Hyane, taking a cigarette from the silver box on the table. "I rather wonder why I have the nerve to see you myself. I've come on a very delicate matter."

There was a silence.

"Indeed?" said Bones a little huskily, and he knew instinctively what that delicate matter was.

"It is about Marguerite," said Mr. Hyane.

Bones inclined his head.

"You see, we have been great pals all our lives," went on Jackson Hyane, pulling steadily at the cigarette—"in fact, sweethearts."

His keen eyes never left the other's face, and he read all he wanted to know.

"I am tremendously fond of Marguerite," he went on, "and I think I am not flattering myself when I say that Marguerite is tremendously fond of me. I haven't been especially fortunate, and I have never had the money which would enable me to offer Marguerite the kind of life which a girl so delicately nurtured should have."

"Very admirable," said Bones, and his voice came to his own ears as the voice of a stranger.

"A few days ago," Mr. Hyane went on, "I was offered a tea plantation for fourteen thousand pounds. The prospects were so splendid that I went to a financier who is a friend of mine, and he undertook to provide the money, on which, of course, I agreed to pay an interest. The whole future, which had been so black, suddenly became as bright as day. I came to Marguerite, as you saw, with the news of my good luck, and asked her if she would be my wife."

Bones said nothing; his face was a mask.

"And now I come to my difficulty, Mr. Tibbetts," said Hyane. "This afternoon Marguerite and I played upon you a little deception which I hope you will forgive."

"Certainly, certainly" mumbled Bones, and gripped the arms of his chair the tighter.

"When I took Marguerite to lunch to-day," said Hyane, "it was to be—married."

"Married!" repeated Bones dully, and Mr. Hyane nodded.

"Yes, we were married at half-past one o'clock to-day at the Marylebone Registry Office, and I was hoping that Marguerite would be able to tell you her good news herself. Perhaps"—he smiled—"it isn't as good news to her as it is to me. But this afternoon a most tragic thing happened."

He threw away his cigarette, rose, and paced the room with agitated strides. He had practised those very strides all that morning, for he left nothing to chance.

"At three o'clock this afternoon I called upon my financier friend, and discovered that, owing to heavy losses which he had incurred on the Stock Exchange, he was unable to keep his promise. I feel terrible, Mr. Tibbetts! I feel that I have induced Marguerite to marry me under false pretences. I had hoped to-morrow morning to have gone to the agents of the estate and placed in their hands the cheque for fourteen thousand pounds, and to have left by the next mail boat for India."

He sank into the chair, his head upon his hands, and Bones watched him curiously.

Presently, and after an effort, Bones found his voice.

"Does your—your—wife know?" he asked.

Jackson shook his head.

"No," he groaned, "that's the terrible thing about it. She hasn't the slightest idea. What shall I tell her? What shall I tell her?"

"It's pretty rotten, old—Mr. Hyane." Bones found his voice after a while. "Deuced rotten for the young miss—for Mrs.—for her."

He did not move from his chair, nor relax his stiff expression. He was hurt beyond his own understanding, frantically anxious to end the interview, but at a loss to find an excuse until his eyes fell upon the clock over the mantelpiece.

"Come back at ten—no, half-past ten, young Mr. . . . awfully busy now. . . see you at half-past ten, eh?"

Mr. Hyane made a graceful exit, and left Bones alone with the shattered fragments of great romance.

So that was why she had gone off in such a hurry, and she had not dared to tell him. But why not? He was nothing to her. . . he would never see her again! The thought made him cold. Never again! Never again! He tried to summon that business fortitude of his, of which he was so proud. He wanted some support, some moral support in this moment of acute anguish. Incidentally he wanted to cry, but didn't.

She ought to have given him a week's notice, he told himself fiercely, than laughed hysterically at the thought. He considered the matter from all its aspects and every angle, and was no nearer to peace of mind when, at half-past ten to the second, Mr. Jackson Hyane returned.

But Bones had formed one definite conclusion, and had settled upon the action he intended taking. Mr. Hyane, entering the study, saw the cheque book on the desk, and was cheered. Bones had to clear his voice several times before he could articulate.

"Mr. Hyane," he said huskily, "I have been thinking matters out. I am a great admirer of yours—of your—of yours—a tremendous admirer of yours, Mr. Hyane. Anything that made her happy, old Mr. Hyane, would make me happy. You see?"

"I see," said Mr. Hyane, and he had the satisfaction of knowing that he, a student of men, had not misread his victim.

"Fourteen thousand pounds," said Bones, turning abruptly to the desk and seizing his pen. "Make it payable to you?"

"You're too kind," murmured Hyane. "Make it an open cheque, Mr. Tibbetts—I have to pay the agents in cash. These Indian merchants are so suspicious."

Bones wrote the cheque rapidly, marked it "Pay Cash," and initialled the corrections, then tore the slip from the book and handed it to the other.

"Of course, Mr. Tibbetts," said Hyane reverentially, "I regard half this as a loan to me and half as a loan to my dear wife. We shall never forget your kindness."

"Rot!" said Bones. "Nonsense! I hope you'll be happy, and will you tell her——" He swallowed something.

There was a faint tinkle of a bell in the hall, and Ali, his servant, poked an ebony face round the corner of the door.

"Sir," he said, "the telephonic apparatus demands conversation."

Bones was glad of the interruption, and, with a muttered apology to his gratified guest, he strode out into the hall. Ali had accustomed himself to answering the telephone, but this time he had not understood the preliminary inquiry from exchange.

"Hello!" said Bones into the transmitter.

"Who's that?"

At the sound of the voice which answered him he nearly dropped the receiver.

"Is that Mr. Tibbetts?"

"Yes," said Bones hoarsely, and his heart beat a wild rataplan.

"I'm speaking from York, Mr. Tibbetts. I wanted to tell you that the key of the safe is in the drawer of my desk—the top drawer."

"That's all right, dear old—dear Mrs. Hyane."

"What is that you say?" asked the voice sharply.

"Congratulations, dear old missus," said Bones. "Hope you'll be awfully happy on your plantation."

"What do you mean?" asked the voice. "Did you call me Mrs. Hyane?"

"Yes," said Bones huskily.

He heard her laugh.

"How ridiculous you are! Did you really think I would ever marry my cousin?"

"But haven't you?" yelled Bones.

"What—married? Absurd! I'm going to Scotland to see about some family matter."

"You're not—not a Mrs.?" asked Bones emphatically.

"And never will be," said the girl. "What does it all mean? Tell me."

Bones drew a long breath.

"Come back by the next train, young miss," he said. "Let that jolly old family affair go to blazes. I'll meet you at the station and tell you everything."

"But—but——" said the girl.

"Do as you're told, young miss!" roared Bones, and hung up the receiver with a seraphic smile.

The door of his study was a thick one, and it was, moreover, protected from outside noises by a large baize door, and the student of men had heard nothing. Bones strode back into the room with a face so changed that Mr. Hyane could not but observe that something remarkable had happened.

"I'm afraid I'm keeping you up, Mr. Tibbetts," he said.

"Not at all," said Bones cheerfully. "Let's have a look at that cheque I gave you."

The other hesitated.

"Let me have a look at it," said Bones, and Mr. Hyane, with a smile, took it from his pocket and handed it to the other.

"Half for you and half for her, eh, dear old thing?" said Bones, and tore the cheque in two. "That's your half," he said, handing one portion to Mr. Hyane.

"What the devil are you doing?" demanded the other angrily, but Bones had him by the collar, and was kicking him along the all-too-short corridor.

"Open the door, Ali!" said Bones. "Open it wide, dear old heathen! Ooff!"

The "Ooff!" was accompanied by one final lunge of Bones's long legs.

At midnight Bones was sitting on the platform at King's Cross, alternately smoking a large pipe and singing tuneless songs. They told him that the next train from York would not arrive until three in the morning.

"That doesn't worry me, old thing. I'll wait all night."

"Expecting somebody, sir?" asked the inquisitive porter.

"Everybody, my dear old uniformed official," said Bones, "everybody!"

Chapter 12

Bones Hits Back

It may be said of Bones that he was in the City, but not of it. Never once had he been invited by the great and awe-inspiring men who dominate the finance of the City to participate in any of those adventurous undertakings which produce for the adventurers the fabulous profits about which so much has been written. There were times when Bones even doubted whether the City knew he was in it.

He never realised his own insignificance so poignantly as when he strolled through the City streets at their busiest hour, and was unrecognised even by the bareheaded clerks who dashed madly in all directions, carrying papers of tremendous importance.

The indifference of the City to Mr. Tibbetts and his partner was more apparent than real. It is true that the great men who sit around the green baize cloth at the Bank of England and arrange the bank rate knew not Bones nor his work. It is equally true that the very important personages who occupy suites of rooms in Lombard Street had little or no idea of his existence. But there were men, and rich and famous men at that, who had inscribed the name of Bones in indelible ink on the tablets of their memory.

The Pole Brothers were shipbrokers, and had little in common, in their daily transactions, with Mr. Harold de Vinne, who specialised in industrial stocks, and knew little more about ships than could be learnt in an annual holiday trip to Madeira. Practically there was no bridge to connect their intellects. Sentimentally, life held a common cause, which they discovered one day, when Mr. Fred Pole met Mr. Harold de Vinne at lunch to discuss a matter belonging neither to the realms of industrialism nor the mercantile marine, being, in fact, the question of Mr. de Vinne leasing or renting Mr. Pole's handsome riverside property at Maidenhead for the term of six months.

They might not have met even under these circumstances, but for the fact that some dispute arose as to who was to pay the gardener. That matter had been amicably settled, and the two had reached the coffee stage of their luncheon, when Mr. de Vinne mentioned the inadvisability—as a rule—of discussing business matters at lunch, and cited a deplorable happening when an interested eavesdropper had overheard certain important negotiations and had most unscrupulously taken advantage of his discovery.

"One of these days," said Mr. de Vinne between his teeth, "I'll be even with that gentleman." (He did not call him a gentleman.) "I'll give him Tibbetts! He'll be sorry he was ever born."

"Tibbetts?" said Mr. Fred Pole, sitting bolt upright. "Not Bones?"

The other nodded and seemed surprised.

"You don't know the dear fellow, do you?" he asked, only he did not use the expression "dear fellow."

"Know him?" said Mr. Fred, taking a long breath. "I should jolly well say I did know him. And my brother Joe knows him. That fellow——"

"That fellow——" began Mr. de Vinne, and for several minutes they talked together in terms which were uncomplimentary to Augustus Tibbetts.

It appeared, though they did not put the matter so crudely, that they had both been engaged in schemes for robbing Bones, and that in the pursuance of their laudable plans they had found themselves robbed by Bones.

Mr. de Vinne ordered another coffee and prepared to make an afternoon of it. They discussed Bones from several aspects and in various lights, none of which revealed his moral complexion at its best.

"And believe me," said Mr. de Vinne at the conclusion of his address for the prosecution, "there's money to be made out of that fellow. Why, I believe he has three hundred thousand pounds."

"Three hundred and forty thousand," said the more accurate Mr. Fred.

"A smart man could get it all," said Harold de Vinne, with conviction. "And when I say a smart man, I mean two smart men. I never thought that he had done anybody but me. It's funny I never heard of your case," he said. "He must have got the best of you in the early days."

Mr. Fred nodded.

"I was his first"—he swallowed hard and added—"mug!"

Mr. de Vinne pulled thoughtfully at his black cigar and eyed the ceiling of the restaurant absent-mindedly.

"There's nobody in the City who knows more about Tibbetts than me," he said. He was weak on the classical side, but rather strong on mathematics. "I've watched every transaction he's been in, and I think I have got him down fine."

"Mind you," said Fred, "I think he's clever."

"Clever!" said the other scornfully. "Clever! He's lucky, my dear chap. Things have just fallen into his lap. It's mug's luck that man has had."

Mr. Fred nodded. It was an opinion which he himself had held and ruminated upon.

"It is luck—sheer luck," continued Mr. de Vinne. "And if we'd been clever, we'd have cleaned him. We'll clean him yet," he said, stroking his chin more thoughtfully than ever, "but it's got to be done systematically."

Mr. Fred was interested. The possibility of relieving a fellow-creature of his superfluous wealth by legitimate means, and under the laws and rules which govern the legal transfer of property, was the absorbing interest of his life.

"It has got to be done cleverly, scientifically, and systematically," said Mr. de Vinne, "and there's no sense in jumping to a plan. What do you say to taking a bit of dinner with me at the Ritz-Carlton on Friday?"

Mr. Fred was very agreeable.

"I'll tell you the strength of Bones," said de Vinne, as they left the restaurant. "He was an officer on the West Coast of Africa. His boss was a man named Sanders, who's left the Service and lives at Twickenham. From what I can hear, this chap Tibbetts worships the ground that Sanders walks on. Evidently Sanders was a big bug in West Africa."

On Friday they resumed their conversation, and Mr. de Vinne arrived with a plan. It was a good plan. He was tremulous with pride at the thought of it, and demanded applause and approval with every second breath, which was unlike him.

He was a man of many companies, good, bad, and indifferent, and, reviewing the enterprises with which his name was associated, he had, without the slightest difficulty, placed his finger upon the least profitable and certainly the most hopeless proposition in the Mazeppa Trading Company. And nothing could be better for Mr. de Vinne's purpose, not, as he explained to Fred Pole, if he had searched the Stock Exchange Year Book from cover to cover.

Once upon a time the Mazeppa Trading Company had been a profitable concern. Its trading stores had dotted the African hinterland thickly. It had exported vast quantities of Manchester goods and Birmingham junk, and had received in exchange unlimited quantities of rubber and ivory. But those were in the bad old days, before authority came and taught the aboriginal natives the exact value of a sixpenny looking-glass.

No longer was it possible to barter twenty pounds' worth of ivory for threepennyworth of beads, and the flourishing Mazeppa Trading Company languished and died. Its managers had grown immensely wealthy from their peculations and private trading, and had come home and were occupying opulent villas at Wimbledon, whilst the new men who had been sent to take their places had been so inexperienced that profits fell to nothing. That, in brief, was the history of the Mazeppa Trading Company, which still maintained a few dilapidated stores, managed by half-castes and poor whites.

"I got most of the shares for a song," confessed Mr. de Vinne. "In fact, I happen to be one of the debenture-holders, and stepped in when things were going groggy. We've been on the point of winding it up—it is grossly over-capitalised—but I kept it going in the hope that something would turn up."

"What is the general idea?" asked Mr. Fred Pole, interested.

"We'll get a managing director," said Mr. de Vinne solemnly. "A man who is used to the handling of natives, a man acquainted with the West Coast of Africa, a man who can organise."

"Bones?" suggested Mr. Fred.

"Bones be—jiggered!" replied de Vinne scornfully. "Do you think he'd fall for that sort of thing? Not on your life! We're not going to mention it to Bones. But he has a pal—Sanders; you've heard of him. He's a commissioner or something on the West Coast, and retired. Now, my experience of a chap of that kind who retires is that he gets sick to death of doing nothing. If we could only get at him and persuade him to accept the managing directorship, with six months a year on the Coast, at a salary of, say, two thousand a year, conditional on taking up six or seven thousand pounds' worth of shares, what do you think would happen?"

Mr. Fred's imagination baulked at the problem, and he shook his head.

"I'll tell you what would happen," said Mr. de Vinne. "It happened once before, when another pal of Bones got let in on a motor car company. Bones fell over himself to buy the shares and control the company. And, mind you, the Mazeppa looks good. It's the sort of proposition that would appeal to a young and energetic man. It's one of those bogy companies that seem possible, and a fellow who knows the ropes would say straight away: 'If I had charge of that, I'd make it pay.' That's what I'm banking on."

"What are the shares worth?" said Fred.

"About twopence net," replied the other brutally. "I'll tell you frankly that I'd run this business myself if I thought there was any chance of my succeeding. But if Bones finds all the shares in one hand, he's going to shy. What I'm prepared to do is this. These shares are worth twopence. I'm going to sell you and a few friends parcels at a shilling a share. If nothing happens, I'll undertake to buy them back at the same price."

A week later Hamilton brought news to the office of Tibbetts and Hamilton, Limited.

"The chief is going back to the Coast."

Bones opened his mouth wide in astonishment.

"Back to the Coast?" he said incredulously. "You don't mean he's chucking jolly old Twickenham?"

Hamilton nodded.

"He's had an excellent offer from some people in the City to control a trading company. By the way, did you ever hear of the Mazeppa Company?" Bones shook his head.

"I've heard of Mazeppa," he said. "He was the naughty old gentleman who rode through the streets of Birmingham without any clothes."

Hamilton groaned.

"If I had your knowledge of history," he said despairingly, "I'd start a bone factory. You're thinking of Lady Godiva, but that doesn't matter. No, I don't suppose you've heard of the Mazeppa Company; it did not operate in our territory."

Bones shook his head and pursed his lips.

"But surely," he said, "dear old Excellency hasn't accepted a job without consulting me?"

Hamilton made derisive noises.

"He fixed it up in a couple of days," he said, after a while. "It doesn't mean he'll be living on the Coast, but he'll probably be there for some months in the year. The salary is good—in fact, it's two thousand a year. I believe Sanders has to qualify for directorship by taking some shares, but the dear chap is enthusiastic about it, and so is Patricia. It is all right, of course. Sanders got the offer through a firm of solicitors."

"Pooh!" said Bones. "Solicitors are nobody."

He learnt more about the company that afternoon, for Sanders called in and gave a somewhat roseate view of the future.

"The fact is, Bones, I am getting stale," he said, "and this looks like an excellent and a profitable occupation."

"How did you get to hear about it, Excellency?". asked Bones.

His attitude was one of undisguised antagonism. He might have been a little resentful that the opportunity had come to Sanders through any other agency than his own.

"I had a letter from the solicitors asking me if the idea appealed to me, and recalling my services on the Coast," said Sanders. "Of course I know very little about the Mazeppa Trading Company, though I had heard of it years gone past as a very profitable concern. The solicitors were quite frank, and told me that business had fallen off, due to inexperienced management. They pointed out the opportunities which existed— the possibilities of opening new stations—and I must confess that it appealed to me. It will mean hard work, but the salary is good."

"Hold hard, Sir and Excellency," said Bones. "What did you have to put up in the way of shares?"

Sanders flushed. He was a shy man, and not given to talking about his money affairs.

"Oh, about five thousand pounds," he said awkwardly. "Of course, it's a lot of money; but even if the business isn't successful, I have a five-year contract with the company, and I get more than my investment back in salary."

That night Bones stayed on after Hamilton had left, and had for companion Miss Marguerite Whitland, a lady in whose judgment he had a most embarrassing faith. He had given her plenty of work to do, and the rhythmical tap-tap of her typewriter came faintly through the door which separated the outer from the inner office.

Bones sat at his desk, his chin in his hand, a very thoughtful young man, and before him was a copy of the latest evening newspaper, opened at the Stock Exchange page. There had been certain significant movements in industrial shares—a movement so interesting to the commentator upon Stock Exchange doings that he had inserted a paragraph to the effect that:

"The feature of the industrial market was the firmness of Mazeppa Trading shares, for which there was a steady demand, the stock closing at 19s. 9d. Mazeppa shares have not been dealt in within the House for many years, and, in fact, it was generally believed that the Company was going into liquidation, and the shares could be had for the price of the paper on which they were printed. It is rumoured in the City that the Company is to be reconstructed, and that a considerable amount of new capital has been found, with the object of expanding its existing business."

Bones read the paragraph many times, and at the conclusion of each reading returned to his reverie. Presently he rose and strolled into the office of his secretary, and the girl looked up with a smile as Bones seated himself on the edge of her table.

"Young miss," he said soberly, "do you ever hear anybody talking about me in this jolly old City?"

"Why, yes," she said in surprise.

"Fearfully complimentarily, dear old miss?" asked Bones carelessly, and the girl's colour deepened.

"I don't think it matters what people say about one, do you?"

"It doesn't matter to me," said Bones, "so long as one lovely old typewriter has a good word for poor old Bones." He laid his hand upon hers, and she suffered it to remain there without protest. "They think I'm a silly old ass, don't they?"

"Oh, no," she said quickly, "they don't think that. They say you're rather unconventional."

"Same thing," said Bones. "Anybody who's unconventional in business is a silly old ass."

He squeezed the hand under his, and again she did not protest or withdraw it from his somewhat clammy grip.

"Dear old darling——" began Bones, but she stopped him with a warning finger.

"Dear old typewriter," said Bones, unabashed, but obedient, "suppose something happened to the clever old Johnny who presides over this office—the brains of the department, if I may be allowed to say so?"

"Captain Hamilton?" said the girl in surprise.

"No, me," said Bones, annoyed. "Gracious Heavens, dear old key-tapper, didn't I say me?"

"Something happen to you?" she said in alarm. "Why, what could happen to you?"

"Suppose I went broke?" said Bones, with the comfortable air of one who was very unlikely to go broke. "Suppose I had terrific and tremendous and cataclysmic and what's-the-other-word losses?"

"But you're not likely to have those, are you?" she asked.

"Not really," said Bones, "but suppose?"

She saw that, for once, when he was speaking to her, his mind was elsewhere, and withdrew her hand. It was a fact that Bones did not seem to notice the withdrawal.

"Poor old Bones, poor old mug!" said Bones softly. "I'm a funny old devil."

The girl laughed.

"I don't know what you're thinking about," she said, "but you never strike me as being particularly funny, or poor, or old, for the matter of that," she added demurely.

Bones stooped down from the table and laid his big hand on her head, rumpling her hair as he might have done to a child.

"You're a dear old Marguerite," he said softly, "and I'm not such a ditherer as you think. Now, you watch old Bones." And, with that cryptic remark, he stalked back to his desk.

Two days after this he surprised Hamilton.

"I'm expecting a visitor to-day, old Ham," he said. "A Johnny named de Vinne."

"De Vinne?" frowned Hamilton. "I seem to know that name. Isn't he the gentleman you had the trouble with over the boots?"

"That's the jolly old robber," said Bones cheerfully. "I've telegraphed and asked him to come to see me."

"About what?" demanded Hamilton.

"About two o'clock," said Bones. "You can stay and see your old friend through, or you can let us have it out with the lad in camera."

"I'll stay," said Hamilton. "But I don't think he'll come."

"I do," said Bones confidently, and he was justified in his confidence, for at two o'clock to the second Mr. de Vinne appeared.

He was bright and cheerful, even genial to Bones, and Bones was almost effusive in his welcome.

"Sit down there in the most comfortable chair, happy old financier," he said, "and open your young heart to old Bones about the Mazeppa Trading Company."

Mr. de Vinne did not expect so direct an attack, but recovered from his surprise without any apparent effort.

"Oh, so you know I was behind that, do you? How the dickens did you find out?"

"Stock Exchange Year Book, dear old thing. Costs umpteen and sixpence, and you can find out everything you want to know about the directors of companies," said Bones.

"By Jove! That's clever of you," said de Vinne, secretly amused, for it was from the Year Book that he expected Bones to make the discovery.

"Now, what's the game, old financial gentleman?" asked Bones. "Why this fabulous salary to friend Sanders and selling this thousands of pounds worth of shares, eh?"

The other shrugged his shoulders.

"My dear chap, it's a business transaction. And really, if I thought you were going to interrogate me on that, I shouldn't have come. Is Mr. Sanders a friend of yours?" he asked innocently.

"Shurrup!" said Bones vulgarly. "You know jolly well he's a friend of mine. Now, what is the idea, young company promoter?"

"It's pretty obvious," replied de Vinne, taking the expensive cigar which Bones had imported into the office for the purpose. "The position is a good one——"

"Half a mo'," said Bones. "Do you personally guarantee Mr. Sanders's salary for five years?"

The other laughed.

"Of course not. It is a company matter," he said, "and I should certainly not offer a personal guarantee for the payment of any salary."

"So that, if the company goes bust in six months' time, Mr. Sanders loses all the money he has invested and his salary?"

The other raised his shoulders again with a deprecating smile.

"He would, of course, have a claim against the company for his salary," he said.

"A fat lot of good that would be!" answered Bones.

"Now, look here, Mr. Tibbetts"—the other leaned confidentially forward, his unlighted cigar between his teeth—"there is no reason in the world why the Mazeppa Company shouldn't make a fortune for the right man. All it wants is new blood and capable direction. I confess," he admitted, "that I have not the time to give to the company, otherwise I'd guarantee a seven per cent. dividend on the share capital. Why, look at the price of them to-day——"

Bones stopped him.

"Any fool can get the shares up to any price he likes, if they're all held in one hand," he said.

"What?" said the outraged Mr. de Vinne. "Do you suggest I have rigged the market? Besides, they're not all in one hand. They're pretty evenly distributed."

"Who holds 'em?" asked Bones curiously.

"Well, I've got a parcel, and Pole Brothers have a parcel."

"Pole Brothers, eh?" said Bones, nodding. "Well, well!"

"Come, now, be reasonable. Don't be suspicious, Mr. Tibbetts," said the other genially. "Your friend's interests are all right, and the shareholders' interests are all right. You might do worse than get control of the company yourself."

Bones nodded.

"I was thinking of that," he said.

"I assure you," said Mr. de Vinne with great earnestness, "that the possibilities of the Mazeppa Trading Company are unlimited. We have concessions from the Great River to the north of the French territory——"

"Not worth the paper they're written on, dear old kidder," said Bones, shaking his head. "Chiefs' concessions without endorsement from the Colonial Office are no good, dear old thing."

"But the trading concessions are all right," insisted the other. "You can't deny that. You understand the Coast customs better than I do. Trading customs hold without endorsement from the Colonial Office."

Bones had to admit that that was a fact.

"I'll think it over," he said. "It appeals to me, old de Vinne. It really does appeal to me. Who own the shares?"

"I can give you a list," said Mr. de Vinne, with admirable calm, "and you'd be well advised to negotiate privately with these gentlemen. You'd probably get the shares for eighteen shillings." He took a gold pencil from his pocket and wrote rapidly a list of names, and Bones took the paper from his hand and scrutinised them.

Hamilton, a silent and an amazed spectator of the proceedings, waited until de Vinne had gone, and then fell upon his partner.

"You're not going to be such a perfect jackass——" he began, but Bones's dignified gesture arrested his eloquence.

"Dear old Ham," he said, "senior partner, dear old thing! Let old Bones have his joke."

"Do you realise," said Hamilton, "that you are contemplating the risk of a quarter of a million? You're mad, Bones!"

Bones grinned.

"Go down to our broker and buy ten thousand shares in old Mazeppa, Ham," he said. "You'll buy them on the market for nineteen shillings, and I've an idea that they're worth about the nineteenth part of a farthing."

"But——" stammered Hamilton.

"It is an order," said Bones, and he spoke in the Bomongo tongue.

"Phew!" said Hamilton. "That carries me a few thousand miles. I wonder what those devils of the N'gombi are doing now?"

"I'll tell you something they're not doing," said Bones. "They're not buying Mazeppa shares."

There were two very deeply troubled people in the office of Tibbetts and Hamilton. One was Hamilton himself, and the other was Miss Marguerite Whitland. Hamilton had two causes for worry. The first and the least was the strange extravagance of Bones. The second—and this was more serious—was the prospect of breaking to Sanders that night that he had been swindled, for swindled he undoubtedly was. Hamilton had spent a feverish hour canvassing City opinion on the Mazeppa Trading Company, and the report he had had was not encouraging. He had, much against his will, carried out the instructions of Bones, and had purchased in the open market ten thousand shares in the Company—a transaction duly noted by Mr. de Vinne and his interested partner.

"He is biting," said that exultant man over the 'phone. "All we have to do is to sit steady, and he'll swallow the hook!"

It was impossible that Marguerite Whitland should not know the extent of her employer's commitments. She was a shrewd girl, and had acquired a very fair working knowledge of City affairs during the period of her employment. She had, too, an instinct for a swindle, and she was panic-stricken at the thought that Bones was marching headlong to financial disaster. Hamilton had gone home to his disagreeable task, when the girl came from her office and stood, her hands clasped behind her, before the desk of the senior partner.

Bones peered up in his short-sighted way.

"Well, young miss?" he said quietly.

"Mr. Tibbetts," she began a little unsteadily, "I'm going to be very impertinent."

"Not at all," murmured Bones.

"I've been with you for some time now," said the girl, speaking rapidly, "and I feel that I have a better right to talk to you than—than——"

"Than anybody in the whole wide world," said Bones, "and that's a fact, dear young Marguerite."

"Yes, yes," she said hurriedly, "but this is something about business, and about—about this deal which you're going into. I've been talking to Captain Hamilton this afternoon, while you were out, and I know it's a swindle."

"I know that, too," said Bones calmly.

"But," said the puzzled girl, "you are putting all your money into it. Mr. Hamilton said that, if this failed, you might be ruined."

Bones nodded. Outwardly calm, the light of battle shone in his eye.

"It's a gamble, dear young typewriter," he said, "a terrific gamble, but it's going to turn out all right for did Bones."

"But Mr. Hamilton said you can't possibly make anything from the property—that it is derelict and worth practically nothing. Only a tenth of the stores are open, and the trading is——"

Bones smiled.

"I'm not gambling on the property," he said softly. "Oh, dear, no, young fiancée, I'm not gambling on the property."

"Then what on earth are you gambling on?" she asked, a little piqued.

"On me," said Bones in the same tone. "On poor old silly ass Bones, and I'm coming through!"

He got up and came across to her and laid his big hand on her shoulder gently.

"If I don't come through, I shan't be a beggar. I shall have enough to build a jolly little place, where we can raise cows and horses and vegetables of all descriptions, dear old typewriter. And if I do come through, we'll still have that same place—only perhaps we'll have more cows and a pig or two."

She laughed, and he raised her smiling lips to his and kissed them.

Mr. de Vinne had dined well and had enjoyed an evening's amusement. He had been to the Hippodrome, and his enjoyment had been made the more piquant by the knowledge that Mr. Augustus Tibbetts had as good as placed ten thousand pounds in his pocket. He was a surprised man, on returning to Sloane Square, to discover, waiting in the hall, his unwilling benefactor.

"Why, Mr. Tibbetts," he said, "this is a great surprise."

"Yes," said Bones, "I suppose it is, old Mr. de Vinne." And he coughed solemnly, as one who was the guardian of a great secret.

"Come in," said Mr. de Vinne, more genial than ever. "This is my little den"—indicating a den which the most fastidious of lions would not have despised. "Sit down and have a cigar, old man. Now, what brings you here to-night?"

"The shares," said Bones soberly. "I've been worrying about the shares."

"Ah, yes," said Mr. de Vinne carelessly. "Why worry about them, dear boy?"

"Well, I thought I might lose the opportunity of buying them. I think there's something to be made out of that property. In fact," said

Bones emphatically, "I'm pretty certain I could make a lot of money if I had control."

"I agree with you," said the earnest Mr. de Vinne.

"Now the point is," said Bones, "I've been studying that list of yours, and it seems to me that the majority of the two hundred and fifty thousand shares issued are either held by you or by one of the Poles—jolly old Joe or jolly old Fred, I don't know which."

"Jolly old Fred," said Mr. de Vinne gravely.

"Now, if there's one person I don't want to meet to-night, or to-morrow, or any other day," said Bones, "it's Pole."

"There's no need for you to meet him," smiled de Vinne.

"In fact," said Bones, with sudden ferocity, "I absolutely refuse to buy any shares from Fred. I'll buy yours, but I will not buy a single one from Fred."

Mr. De Vinne thought rapidly.

"There's really no reason," he said carelessly. "As a matter of fact, I took over Fred's shares to-night, or the majority of them. I can let you have—let me see"—he made a rapid calculation—"I can let you have a hundred and eighty thousand shares at nineteen and nine."

"Eighteen shillings," said Bones firmly, "and not a penny more."

They wrangled about the price for five minutes, and then, in an outburst of generosity, Mr. de Vinne agreed.

"Eighteen shillings it shall be. You're a hard devil," he said. "Now, shall we settle this in the morning?"

"Settle it now," said Bones. "I've a contract note and a cheque book."

De Vinne thought a moment.

"Why, sure!" he said. "Let's have your note."

Bones took a note from his pocket, unfolded it, and laid it on the table, then solemnly seated himself at Mr. de Vinne's desk and wrote out the cheque.

His good fortune was more than Mr. de Vinne could believe. He had expected Bones to be easy, but not so easy as this.

"Good-bye," said Bones. He was solemn, even funereal.

"And, my friend," thought Mr. de Vinne, "you'll be even more solemn before the month's out."

He saw Bones to the door, slapped him on the back, insisted on his taking another cigar, and stood outside on the pavement of Cadogan Square and watched the rear lights of Bones's car pass out of sight. Then he went back to his study telephone and gave a number. It was the number of Mr. Fred Pole's house, and Fred Pole himself answered the call.

"Is that you, Pole?"

"That's me," said the other, and there was joy in his voice.

"I say, Pole," chuckled de Vinne, "I shall save you a lot of trouble."

"What do you mean?" asked the other.

"I've sold Bones my shares and yours too."

There was a deep silence.

"Did you hear me?" asked de Vinne.

"Yes, I heard you," said the voice, so strange that de Vinne scarcely recognised it. "How many did you sell?" asked Pole.

"A hundred and eighty thousand. I thought I could easily fix it with you."

Another silence.

"What did Bones say to you?"

"He told me he wouldn't do any more business with you."

"Good Heavens!" groaned Pole, and added, "Gracious Heavens!"

"Why, what's the matter?" asked de Vinne quickly, scenting danger.

"That's what he said to me," moaned the other. "Just hang on. I'll be round in a quarter of an hour."

Mr. Fred Pole arrived under that time, and had a dreadful story to unfold. At nine o'clock that evening Bones had called upon him and had offered to buy his shares. But Bones had said he would not under any circumstances——

"Buy my shares?" said de Vinne quickly.

"Well, he didn't exactly say that," said Fred. "But he gave me to understand that he'd rather buy the shares from me than from anybody else, and I thought it was such an excellent idea, and I could fix it up with you on the telephone, so I sold him——"

"How many?" wailed de Vinne.

"A hundred and fifty thousand," said Mr. Fred, and the two men stared at one another.

De Vinne licked his dry lips.

"It comes to this," he said. "Between us we've sold him three hundred and thirty thousand shares. There are only two hundred and fifty thousand shares issued, so we've got to deliver eighty thousand shares that are non-existent or be posted as defaulters."

Another long pause, and then both men said simultaneously, as though the thought had struck them for the first time:

"Why, the fellow's a rogue!"

The next morning they called upon Bones, and they were with him for half an hour; and when they went, they left behind them, not only the cheques that Bones had given them, but another cheque for a most substantial amount as consideration.

That night Bones gave a wonderful dinner-party at the most expensive hotel in London. Sanders was there, and Patricia Sanders, and Hamilton, and a certain Vera, whom the bold Bones called by her Christian name, but the prettiest of the girls was she who sat on his right and listened to the delivery of Bones's great speech in fear and trembling.

"The toast of the evening, dear old friends," said Bones, "is Cupidity and Cupid. Coupled with the names of the Honourable de Vinne and my young and lovely typewriter—my friend and companion in storm and stress, the only jolly old lady, if I may be allowed to say so, that has stirred my young heart"—he caught Patricia Sanders's accusing eye, coughed, and added—"in Europe!"

THE END

A Note About the Author

Edgar Wallace (1875–1932) was a London-born writer who rose to prominence during the early twentieth century. With a background in journalism, he excelled at crime fiction with a series of detective thrillers following characters J.G. Reeder and Detective Sgt. (Inspector) Elk. Wallace is known for his extensive literary work, which has been adapted across multiple mediums, including over 160 films. His most notable contribution to cinema was the novelization and early screenplay for 1933's *King Kong*.

A Note from the Publisher

Spanning many genres, from non-fiction essays to literature classics to children's books and lyric poetry, Mint Edition books showcase the master works of our time in a modern new package. The text is freshly typeset, is clean and easy to read, and features a new note about the author in each volume. Many books also include exclusive new introductory material. Every book boasts a striking new cover, which makes it as appropriate for collecting as it is for gift giving. Mint Edition books are only printed when a reader orders them, so natural resources are not wasted. We're proud that our books are never manufactured in excess and exist only in the exact quantity they need to be read and enjoyed.

bookfinity™

Discover more of your favorite classics with Bookfinity™.

- Track your reading with custom book lists.
- Get great book recommendations for your personalized Reader Type.
- Add reviews for your favorite books.
- AND MUCH MORE!

Visit **bookfinity.com** and take the fun Reader Type quiz to get started.

Enjoy our classic and modern companion pairings!

Classic & Modern

9 781513 266404